REUNION

BY THE

LAKE

REUNION BY THE LAKE

A NOVEL

JAMES GILBERT

atmosphere press

Published by Atmosphere Press

Cover design by Kevin Stone

Atmospherepress.com

"...do not go gentle..."

—Dylan Thomas

CHAPTER 1

"What exactly do you intend to tell them?"

"I'm not sure how I'll say it," Richard replied. "I haven't made a plan yet. But they need to know."

"So perhaps you're expecting them to read your mind? Or maybe you think it's somehow written on your frown?"

"I'll find an opportunity; or make one," he said, looking out over the dark water of the lake. He was still for a minute and then continued softly: "Have you ever noticed that the sky can be completely bright at sunset, full of colors: reds and blues and oranges, but the lake remains as black as night?"

"Are you deliberately changing the subject?" she interrupted.

"Obviously, I am, yes. Because I'm not in the mood to argue. And doesn't it look as if the sun pulls a shadow across the earth as it retreats to the horizon?"

"So, I suppose you will make them guess? Or are you reconsidering?"

"You're damned persistent, Grace. Of course I'll tell them, but in my own sweet time. And no, I've decided; it's final. They'll get what they deserve."

Grace looked out over the lake, as if something had caught her attention in the fading light.

She sighed, folded her hands in her lap, and made a vague sound as if she were agreeing with herself—the way she always did when she was exasperated or troubled by the severity of her husband—by his inflexibility and evasions. She was surprised that she had spoken so abruptly to him: was it his weakness, she wondered? Did that demand some sudden shift in the balance between them?

They sat quietly as the colors of the sunset darkened into streaks of grey clouds set against a momentary silvery sky.

"It'll be chilly in a minute," she said. "I think we ought to go in."

"Not just yet. A minute longer. I won't have many more of these."

"You shouldn't talk that way!"

"Why? Am I being too honest? Borrowed time.... Did you ever think about what that means? Well, I have. And borrowed from what or who?" he asked.

"I believe it's from yourself," she said, abruptly.

"Yes, perhaps you're right. Just a confusing way of saying you hope to get some sort of extension, some temporary renewal."

"A reprieve."

"But not a remission."

He looked at her curiously, as if the shadow of evening that fell on her face was a disguise. Did he know her? After so many years.

"I don't mean to..." he said. "I'm very tired."

"It's all right. I understand."

They were silent again; night noises were emerging

around them: the creaking call and response of frogs first, and then the rustle of the wind as the cold, damp air sank down from the hill behind the pines. Later, he thought, if he were awake, as he often was now, and listening through the open window, he might hear the stamping hoofs of a deer or the faint swish of grass as some other nocturnal animal scurried by the house.

"Well, I'm going in," she said, "before I get a chill. And you should too."

"Just another minute. And I want you to remind me about the times they're arriving."

"Have you forgotten what I said already?"

"Yes. Would I ask otherwise?"

"Maybe, but you might," she said. "Well, Deck will be here first, tomorrow sometime, early probably, then Nick, and then, of course, Seth and Lee; they said whenever they can manage. By this weekend they'll all be here."

"I would hope so," he said, standing up and leaning against the back of his chair. "I paid for their tickets."

"Not Seth's, no, you didn't. He's driving. And certainly not Deck. Just Nick."

"No, I suppose you're right. At least there's some independence in this family! Enough to finance their own way."

"I hate to say this, but I'm not sure Nick would come if you didn't."

He looked out again over the lake as if he had heard the splash of a jumping fish, or a duck landing. Finally, he said:

"Sometimes I think I shouldn't have asked them to come. I mean, they could always read the obituary. And then, of course, tear into town eager for the reading of the will."

"OK. That's enough of that. It's done and they're coming—you know you wanted that. Let's go inside now, Richard. There's a chill." She did not add that he must be looking forward to the drama of the moment when he revealed the potent words on a legal document that would change all of their lives.

She helped him to stand, and they walked slowly up the brick path toward the house. The darkness had brought out a flickering cloud of fireflies that winked their momentary come-hither signals in tiny flashes of cold yellow light. In front of them, the dark outline of the house deepened the twilight shadows to pitch. But when they reached the deck, an automatic light flashed on, and suddenly the buzzing night retreated just beyond the luminous circle that it cast.

"Do you want some help?" she said.

"Yes. Just give me your arm. It's those damned steps."

"Of course," she said, holding out a crooked elbow for him to grab onto. "And I'll make some dinner if you're up to it."

"Just a glass of wine, if there's any, or something stronger. I haven't got much appetite tonight."

"You need to eat, Richard. The doctor said..."

"I don't care what that damned fool said. What's the point, anyway? Keep up my strength? And for what? Don't they realize it when they're talking banalities?

"Everything he says to me must come straight out of the *Physicians' Guide to Platitudes*. I'll bet it's a medical school graduation gift. Certainly a lot more useful than a diploma! The only time I could actually trust him was when I forced him to tell me the truth. Even then, wrapped it up so tight in circumlocutions at first that I could barely get it untangled. Until I just demanded to know, outright: 'How much time?' And then he hemmed and hawed some more until I asked him again, and then he finally told me. Another stroke any day. End of story! End of me."

As they entered the large living room through a sliding glass door, Grace switched on the lights, illuminating the warm yellow walls, the fieldstone fireplace, and the two large oriental rugs covering most of the gleaming plank floor.

"Why don't you sit down while I make us something to eat," she said, guiding him toward the leather easy chair where he had spent so many evenings in recent years, since his retirement, reading or writing briefs on oversized yellow pads.

"No, not there, not tonight," he said, waving away her hand and making his way toward the couch that faced the large picture window. It was a new spot for him where he could watch the days descend into night.

"All right," she said quickly, and moved toward the kitchen so he wouldn't see the tears in her eyes. Once, she thought, he had been devoted to the other chair, the one he had occupied almost every night for the last twenty years or so. Ever since they bought this rambling house by the lake. She guessed why he avoided it now, or she thought she understood that it brought back too many memories of all the active days he had spent here since leaving the Chicago law firm—to become a small town lawyer who only took the cases he enjoyed. But disease—dying, to be frank about it—she realized, could make you a stranger in your own house. And bitter. Perhaps that was normal. It was certain that his outbursts were a clumsy protest against the doctor's announcement of this unwelcome verdict.

She too, had been making little alterations and accommodations to his infirmity, but so many now that their accumulation seemed to change everything between them. They had been obliged to remove the double bed where they had slept together for how many years she didn't know. And they purchased twins. He had called his "the last place I'll ever sleep." Trying it out for size the afternoon it had been placed in their bedroom, he called it his hospital bed, his gurney. He once even suggested that they sleep in separate rooms, but she wouldn't hear of it, even if, during the night, he moaned and tossed and turned. She had explained that these disturbances were comforting to her, and reassurances of an odd sort. So he just shrugged and said, "OK—it's up to you."

In the beginning, being witness to his anger and bitterness had deeply confused her. Her own parents had passed away in silent acceptance—at least that's how she remembered it. But for Richard, it seemed as if he couldn't let go—or recognize that he would no longer be able to control the world and the people around him. Maybe, she thought, that was why the will had become so important to him because it was an extension of himself through time, giving him a final grip on all their futures. She wanted to tell him that she understood, but she was afraid that he would mistake her motives and accuse her of interfering.

In the kitchen, she took down two plates from the china cabinet and rummaged through the refrigerator for the salads she had purchased the day before. Not knowing what he would eat, she made a careful arrangement on his: egg salad, humus and chips, and tabbouleh in three distinct mounds. Looking at her work reminded her of preparing meals for her three sons. She had always tried to make dinner a kind of game for them, and now she found herself doing the same for him. But she knew she shouldn't make a comparison like that, even if it seemed right.

When she thought about it, she realized she had done nothing to prepare for this phase, this moment in their lives—not, of course, the food or the drinks or however they slept or didn't sleep together. But his dependency on her. Whoever does? she wondered, absently. Without looking, she reached up to take a glass from the cabinet, but her grip slipped, and it crashed into the sink, breaking into long, sharp slivers. Staring at the pieces, she hesitated, considering if they could be mended, but then she picked them up gingerly, one by one, and discarded them into the trash. How strange that these shards made her think about their incongruous family, this fragmented clan with its sharp personalities, this brittle association that was now about to come back together after how many years. She couldn't remember the last time they had all been together, except that she knew it had made everyone uncomfortable.

But this reunion would be different from any other. For so long, and as far back as she could remember, she had willingly accepted her role as his wife and mother and the diminished partner in their marriage. She had always been the one to urge compromise, to deflect his rigid ways, inserting herself as the intermediary between him and his sons. She had not, until recently, asked herself if she had ever wanted anything different. It had just never occurred to her. But so often now, when he reached out to her, when, in effect, their roles had reversed and he leaned on her, she was surprised at how easily this new strength came to her. But was it what she wanted? She wasn't sure; and there hadn't been time to consider all the possibilities. But she did wonder if she could accommodate herself to this strange and confusing interlude before he would be gone.

Walking back into the living room, she asked him:

"Do you prefer eating in here? I can open up a folding table, or in the dining room?"

"Whatever..."

"Then it's the dining room. I'll set your place. Come in when you're ready."

She busied herself with arranging the table and waited for him, noticing his careful, slow movements when he pulled himself up, and the way he edged, cautiously grabbing onto one piece of furniture after another for support as he approached. It looked to her as if his legs were almost too heavy to lift. He had so much difficulty that he just slid his feet along the carpet and lurched toward her. For a moment, she thought she ought to help him into his chair, but stopped herself, thinking that he would probably just push her away. It continued to make him furious to play the invalid's role, even though he was exactly that. So odd, she thought, that he had accepted the verdict of death and demanded to hear the unblemished truth without euphemisms, but he refused to give in to any of its preliminaries.

"Some of your favorites," she said. "Do try to eat something."

"I will," he said, taking his fork in his right hand. He managed to balance a small portion of salad, but it trembled off before he could reach his mouth.

She said nothing and pretended not to notice when he fumbled for the large spoon she had placed next to his plate. His frustration was almost palpable. And yet, as hard as she tried, she couldn't feel sorry for him. There was too much anger in him and in her, too. Anger that he was dying; but, for her, especially anger at what he was about to do and say to his children. She couldn't help but share a feeling of resentment.

"Do you really plan to go through with it?" she asked, knowing that the question would frustrate him. But she couldn't help herself. There was still time and he could change if he wanted. If she could persuade him.

He looked intently at her, and she wondered for a moment if it was hatred she saw in his eyes or merely the surprise of a sudden pain.

"Of course. Do I have a choice?"

"Not that, Richard!" She couldn't bring herself to say the word: "You know what I mean."

"I've told you a hundred times," he said. "Why must I repeat myself? Yes. I mean to exit this world, knowing that I've made the right decisions about what I'm leaving behind."

"But it's so cruel and judgmental to leave them so little. I still can't believe you're serious," she said. She wanted to say that he couldn't reach out after death and shape their lives as he had always tried to do. But she didn't. Surely he understood that.

"Don't worry, you know you'll be provided for. You know that. I'd never—"

"I don't mean that, Richard," she interrupted. "Not at all. I know. Of course. But so stingy with them. Have you thought of the consequences?"

"Yes, and that's the point, isn't it? The consequences. They need to stand tall, Grace. On their own. And not depend on me. It's for their own good. They have their own lives now. And money would just be a diversion, something that tarnishes ambition. A silly crutch. A corruption. I've tried to live my life that way, not dependent on anyone else. And I want that for them, too."

"I suppose you can't you see me?" she said finally, turning to him.

"What? Of course I can, yes. What are you asking?"

"Can't you see that you've never been alone? Where do you think I've been all these years and doing what? Am I just a bystander, cook and laundress? Your patient admirer? Do you really think you did everything on your own?"

Richard shifted in his chair and glanced down at the food in front of him. He started to reach across the table for her hand, but hesitated:

"I'm sorry. I didn't mean what that sounded like. Of course, of course! But I'm talking about our sons. I think it would disrupt their lives in terrible ways if they had a sudden fortune. It would soften them. I'll always believe that. Listen, Grace, it's not that I don't love them, but if you're honest, truly willing to consider what they've made of themselves so far, it's not much, is it?"

"Who are you to say that, Richard? What gives you the right to judge?" she said softly.

"The simple reality is that I'm their father, and I have this one last chance to push them out of the nest and make them soar on their own wings and not depend on mine."

She sighed, folded her hands in her lap, and made a vague sound as if she were trying to retrieve words that she had spoken to him. She was surprised that she had spoken so harshly to him again: was it his weakness, she wondered? Was that another signal of some sudden shift in the balance between them? But she was determined to continue.

“And why then can't you just divide the rest equally among them? Why do you insist on unequal shares... and so meager?”

“Because they're not equal—equally deserving.”

“But how can you make such a determination?” She did not add *in your condition*. “There's still time to reconsider, isn't there? For the sake of fairness.”

“Time? I don't know. Time? Is there time?” He looked almost amused at his intentional misunderstanding:

“Do you know that when you're dying,” he continued, “the only thing you ever think about is time, the merciful portion that's granted to you? When every day is like the gift of rebirth. And every nightfall is a rehearsal of death—like you're practicing up for when the shroud falls.”

She looked away, not wanting to see the momentary expression on his face: would it be a bitter smile, anguish, pain, a grimace? Or sadness? Or maybe this was just a sardonic joke. She wouldn't put it past him. So often, now, he evaded answering her, as if she was interrupting his private monologue, and what he said made no sense.

Over the last few months, ever since the diagnosis, she had tried to remember him as his former self—the handsome young man she had married and grown old with. He had always been a person prone to smart, cutting, funny remarks—he had an uncanny ability to probe the weakness in others and could then laugh about it in a way that you couldn't tell if it was cruel or kind. But now he had turned this caustic wit on himself. This man of so many paradoxes. So much of what remained of that person seemed to be his rigidity and resignation, as if by holding himself tightly, and not admitting to any of the strange, new emotions he felt, he could evade the end by denying any weakness in himself—pretending, at least, to control the things he saw as weakness. She wondered sometimes if this had to do with the way the law had seeped into his body, replacing the soft marrow of his bones with something rigid and unnatural. Damn the cold objectivity of law, she thought.

"Maybe you're just feeling sorry for yourself?" she said, even though she knew she shouldn't be so direct. But the time for nuance between them had long since passed, and she had abandoned her caution. She put down her fork and stared at his face for a moment, trying to glimpse the person she had known beneath this mask of old age. The strong features were still there—the quick brown eyes, the straight nose, the high cheek bones—visible despite the deposit of soft, heavy flesh lined with tiny, broken blood vessels that gave his face a permanent flushed look.

"Not at all," he said, finally, uncomfortable under her searching glance: "I just want to get this visit over with as soon as possible. I'm not looking forward to it, despite what you think."

"But I'm sure that you are. I know you are. You have everything planned out, every detail, every word."

"Only because it has to be done. They need to know that my legacy to them is in their best interests. My last gift to them."

She interrupted, now determined to change the subject—she had had enough of his obstinacy:

"Did I tell you that Deck called to say he'll arrive tomorrow mid-morning or a bit later? He didn't say if he's bringing someone or not. Just that he would be driving down from Chicago. He didn't tell me much, but then he never does. That boy has always been mysterious about his life. Never says much."

"You're right. I think he loves to spring things on us, to astonish us. Except tomorrow night, when they are all gathered, I'll be the one to amaze."

"Maybe he gets his weakness for drama from you, Richard? Have you thought of that? I mean, what you are going to tell them will be both terrible and upsetting. I hate this. This spectacle you've got planned. And, I'm only going to say this once more and then I'll hold my tongue and you can do anything you want. But I fear that the way you've allotted what you're leaving them will create terrible animosity between them. Is that what you want?"

She stood and picked up her plate: "That's all I have to say to you. I'm done now."

"You think they're jealous of each other? Because if they are, I've got nothing to do with that," he replied. "I won't be creating something that isn't already present. Where have you been while they were growing up?"

"Where have you been?" she said quietly.

Neither of them ventured another word until Richard stood carefully, gripping the arms of his chair to pull himself up.

"You wouldn't mind pouring me a drink, would you? My hand shakes too much. Couldn't eat anything, and drinking is hard enough."

"Of course," she said, putting down her plate and glancing at the cabinet on the wall behind her. "The usual?"

"With an ice cube. And yourself?"

"Yes. I'll bring the glasses into the living room. Can you manage?"

"Probably."

She retreated to the kitchen, carrying her dish and his untouched dinner and shoveled it into the trash bin beneath the sink. As she rinsed the plates, she wondered why she was still trying to change his mind about the will, why she picked at the edges of his determination when she knew he was adamant and would never give in. She had to keep reminding herself that his physical weakness and his decline had done nothing to weaken his resolve: this broken man with an unbroken determination.

Entering the living room, Richard eased himself onto the couch, balancing with his right hand on the arm and slowly dropping onto the seat. He thought he might reach over and turn on the lamp, but decided to sit in the semi-dark for the moment. As he looked around, it reminded him, for no good reason that he could imagine, of the first time they had looked at the house. He remembered that during the afternoon showing he hadn't realized the possibilities until they began to emerge, gradually, like a slow, brightening illumination, as they toured each room with the garrulous real estate agent.

"Such a perfect place for a long retirement," she had bubbled on after they finished their visit. She continued to talk as she swept a leathery hand in a semi-circle as if she had to prompt their eyes to admire every corner of the living room where they were standing.

"And there's the lake and a private dock. Of course you'll get a boat. Almost everyone around here has one. Or you can just fish over the edge if you want. And the sunsets! Scrumptious! Glorious! Lots of bedrooms for when your children visit. I'm right about that, aren't I: three sons? And how many grandchildren? How wonderful," she added, answering her own question before they could object.

He said nothing but scowled at her for pretending she could anticipate his retirement days, instructing him, as if he didn't know any better, about how to enjoy his surroundings or spend his time. He looked to Grace for some agreement with his contempt for this unsolicited sales pitch—unnecessary because they had already decided—and worse, because somehow the words in her mouth sullied the pleasures he anticipated.

But his wife's look had been a mute refusal to be drawn into his displeasure, or his anger. It was just like her to be accommodating and friendly when a caustic remark would silence the agent and allow him his own private contemplation of the years to come. Her indulgent smile told him to remain silent.

They hadn't hesitated to buy this house on the lake. It was located in a relatively new development around an artificial body of water, fed by damming up the meandering Seminole Creek. Their property was almost an acre—mostly lawn and a few tall river birch trees with their shaggy bark and filigree green foliage. All the new houses were situated on large tracts of land running down to the water, separated far enough apart to maintain a friendly privacy, although none was as large as theirs.

Not that their old house in the suburb south of Chicago hadn't been pleasant or large enough. But Richard had wanted something different, not because he disliked that location, but he had insisted that retirement should mean a change of venue. And yet, as it turned out—and he hadn't told her—he certainly did not intend to cut himself off from the law. It had settled into his bones, and an occasional case that didn't involve a court appearance—some will or a contract—was enough to keep him in the practice. Not that Grace approved. She didn't. She had wanted him to cut ties with legal matters entirely. Possibly, he suspected, because she was jealous. Or maybe she just wanted his abiding attention. But she had hoped that their lives would amend.

In fact, something had changed profoundly after they had moved into the new house. He had come to suspect that relinquishing his partnership at the firm had altered the dynamics of their marriage, and the terms of their relationship, even if he was not inclined to often admit it. Theirs had never been a contract between equivalents, but he did not realize the degree to which he would increasingly come to depend upon her and allow her to arrange their day, especially now with his illness. She did so enthusiastically, and he sometimes wondered if that was what she had anticipated and wanted all along.

It had become apparent to him that they had become entirely changed persons living together now for the first time without any of the freshness of novelty and reckless passion (long gone) and, he feared, without much love. Maybe, he mused, that had happened gradually, becoming obvious only when they moved to the new house.

So this was what growing old together meant, he thought. Uncomfortable for a moment, he shifted his position on the couch and tried to see into the dining room if she was coming.

When he first heard that saying, it sounded as ominous as it had turned out to be—only different and wholly unexpected. He hadn't realized or thought, until lately, that aging with someone simply meant that life would become a routine interrupted by moments of noticeable decline, a falling away until the essence of a relationship meant the increasing dependence upon each other and the androgyny of two sexless bodies bound together in greying frailty. Was it a slow dying of everything that was the meaning?

And he had finally come to understand that growing old together meant diminishing alongside someone, but each with a different and unequal pace. That was the surprise! Somehow, she seemed to accept her situation and thrive, whereas his aging was measured only in brief plateaus followed by a sudden pitch into further decline. The worst part, and the unexpected change, had been the disappearance of boundaries, and the cloistered spaces that he had so carefully guarded his whole life, just like the expanse he had purchased for privacy around their house. But now, even his body and all its functions had become public objects, pried and prodded by doctors, monitored on charts and graphs, and shared and worried over by his wife. Even worse, he knew he was the whispered object of commentary among friends and family.

Most surprisingly, his weakness appeared to give her a new kind of strength in their relationship, and although she tried to be careful and evade the sharp edges of his moods, this insidious transfer of power grieved him, and made him lash out, sometimes in anger that he no longer tried to control. He had frequently complained to her that he wanted it to be over, to rush into oblivion, but now that it soon would be all he wanted was enough time to set everything right; to explain and justify himself. He believed it was his duty to exercise this one final influence over the lives of his sons and leave them the just legacy that they each deserved.

Grace turned on the light as she entered, and suddenly the gloom was dissolved as the familiar room around him became visible: the piano in the corner that she had once played, and on which Nick began his first music lessons, the couches, the pictures set in silver frames of each of his sons, the rich, somber colors of the oriental rugs that had been in his family for many years.

"I'll put your drink down here," she said, setting the squat whiskey glass on the table in front of him.

"Cheers," he said, picking it up, but without looking at her.

"I've made the final arrangements," she said.

"That sounds rather bleak! Aren't you rushing things a bit?"

"Oh, you," she laughed. "No, I mean about the dinner, when they're all finally here."

"And for how many?"

"Well, if I know Deck, he's sure to bring someone. Sometimes I think he's afraid to face us alone, or, for that matter, his brothers. Moral courage gained from making us uncomfortable by imposing a stranger on us, I guess. Makes us mind our manners!"

"And Nick? Alone as always, I presume?"

"Unless he brings his cello. I wish he would. I'd love to hear him play again. It's been so long."

"And, of course, Seth and Lee—on their own clock. I suppose you're right, about Deck, that is," he continued. "I've never been able to understand what it is about him. So successful in the world... brags about it, anyway. I don't know how many thousands of dollars he earns a year. But here, here at home, he's just silent and brooding, as if he had retreated into that photo over there, watching us, always disapproving and ready to criticize."

"Are you saying, then, that you understand your other two sons, Richard? Because, to be frank, I have a hard time with both of them too, especially Seth."

"No, of course not. Nick? Single? Why is that? He's always so mysterious about his life. Rarely talks about himself, and when he does, he just lifts a tiny corner and lets us peek under to see only what he wants us to see, just about what you might tell a stranger. Of course we know about him. As if it were some great secret that he has to keep private. Maybe you can deal with him better than me. I mean his music and all. I wonder. Did you see some talent in him that everyone else has missed? Were you the one to convince him to settle for that pathetic career of his?"

"Don't be so harsh, Richard," she said, sitting down opposite him. "Who ever understands their own children. What we wish for them is never who they really become. They will always be part strangers to us and different from our ambition for them. Sometimes it gets confusing to sort out the reality."

"Well, in his case, I think the reality is obvious enough. Nick only has enough talent to give lessons to beginners. Little girls with pink bows in their hair and pale, effeminate young boys. But anyone who has real ability will move on up and away quick enough. Find another, better teacher.."

"Why do you say that?"

"It's what he told me once, or rather implied. Long ago."

"There's nothing wrong in what he does."

"Except his lack of ambition. His acceptance of mediocrity."

"But he's tried out. In competitions, I mean. Several times in fact. I know that last year he almost got a position with the Buffalo Philharmonic. He told me he played his very best in years."

"And he didn't get it—right? Are you surprised?" he said, taking another sip of his drink and setting it down carefully:

"Probably went to someone much younger: a prospect, which he clearly is not. What kind of life is 'almost's and maybe's and next times?'"

"Have you considered that he likes what he does? Have you thought of that? Why do you have to interfere? To judge him?"

"Quite clearly I didn't interfere enough. We let him do what he wanted with his life instead of guiding him."

"What you think of as guidance, Richard, can be a very tight space to squeeze through. And over and against all the rough patches of your disapproval! And you think you can change all that now?"

"So you think it's my fault that he's a failure?"

"Only partly," she said, reaching for her glass. "I'll take some credit too. If he really is that. Maybe he feels he's making a contribution. You know you are a hard comparison."

He picked up his glass and tilted it toward her, clumsily, almost spilling the liquid that remained: "I'll take any compliment I can get," he said. "Anyway, what about Seth and Lee? Any definitive word from them—as if anything in their lives was for sure!"

"I haven't heard yet," she said after a long silence.

"Oh, I suppose they'll be here, no doubt; whenever there's the scent of money," he said, setting his glass down abruptly. "But on their own time. Just won't tell us when. He probably doesn't even know himself."

"Yes, I'm certain they'll be here, too," she said absently. "They always manage. But I think you're wrong about money. Ever since he got religion, he's changed. No, not any more; money's the last thing he's interested in now."

"Maybe. But he's still Seth. That means they'll arrive on their own time, of course. Fifty years old and he has the responsibility of a twelve year old."

"Please, Richard. You mustn't be so critical; sometimes you're so unfair. I don't know why you have to criticize them. I understand that they upset you, and you wish they had achieved the things you approve of, but just once, given the circumstances, couldn't you be understanding?"

He didn't answer because he had no words to express the doubts he had begun to feel, and those he refused to confess to her. It had once been easy to repeat all the things he had long said to his sons, to categorize and explain each of their failures. Of course, it was for their own good. He had meant to inspire them and prod them. But he wondered now, after so many futile years of trying to change and shape them, to mold the stubborn clay, did he have the strength to continue judging them? Recently—and more and more—he had begun to feel that he had treated them harshly, too harshly and that for all his trying, he might be responsible for the very failures in them that he criticized. And yet, he knew, or he thought he understood, that if he relinquished exercising the determined force he had always been in their lives, if he gave up and softened that part of him he believed was truly himself, the tough fiber of his very core would collapse, and he would just be another frail old man, with thin grey hair, in a paisley bathrobe and fuzzy slippers, wandering painfully from room to room in this house of expectant death.

It took all his energy to remain himself, and be the father he had always tried to be. But there were times when he was not sure that he still possessed the strength for that. His weak heart had forced a strange rebirth, threatening the sinews of the person he had carefully created, revealing something in him that was surprising and disturbing and soft and pliable, which he struggled to deny.

Perhaps, he thought, that is why he had shaped his will with such care: it amounted to a kind of brief, an advance obituary of himself, as he had once been and would be only for a short time more, and the way he wanted to be remembered.

"You're awfully silent," his wife said, standing up to remove his glass. "Do you want another?"

"Yes, I think I do."

"Fine. I'll just be a minute," she said, walking back through the dining room into the kitchen where she had left the bottle on the counter.

CHAPTER 2

She stared at the dirty dinner dishes in the sink for a moment, hesitated, and then slid onto a stool next to the kitchen island and sighed. It was not in exasperation or fatigue, but at the thought of his words. All those years of being with him had drained her. It was strange to think—but probably true—that living with this difficult man, who was so set in his ways and so sure of himself, this affiliated life that had become her life as she sometimes thought of it—this had somehow diminished her. Not that she would have traded her years for something or someone else.

But there were times, like tonight, when she realized how important they were, and yet what an obstacle their three sons had always been between them and their happiness. Of course she didn't resent them. How could she? They were hers, her own sons... except, of course, for Seth. Seth. But she and Richard had always disagreed so profoundly about them—he critical and she forever defending and finding excuses for them. And this had shaped their marriage into an ongoing argument that went unresolved. But ironically, it had also been one of the things that bound them together during their roughest times.

She knew she ought to pour him another drink and return to the living room right away, and that he would be impatient, and perhaps he would call out to her. But she remained sitting at the kitchen table instead. He could wait.

She looked around the room that she had carefully planned and outfitted. It was her room, and she had made it her retreat, and a place where she often sat, alone, like now, just thinking. Somewhere she had read that if you don't try to remember the past and relive its details and emotions, it would gradually fade and die out, leaving you with nothing but its empty traces. And that seemed right. To remember had become an almost alien and disturbing preoccupation. And yet....

Lately, she had wanted to sit and think and revisit that time, so many years ago, when Richard had revealed something surprising and profound and completely unexpected about himself. She tried to recall every word and every gesture and how she had felt and what they had said to each other: even the color of the room, the noises and smells. Everything. Because he had done something so strange and unusual, and at a time of her crushing grief, something so gentle and caring, that she would always be grateful to him, even though this startling and miraculous gesture had eventually turned out badly. Or not badly, exactly, but as the beginning of never-ending contention and difficulty between them.

Until that momentous day, she remembered, she hadn't actually realized what he truly felt for her. Of course, they had exchanged words of endearment, but somehow, up until then, these seemed insubstantial. Their marriage had been more or less inevitable as an attachment of best friends. They had grown up in the midst of close family ties and it had, forever, she thought, and in both families it had always been assumed, that theirs would be a perfect match.

When he went away to law school upstate, she waited for his haphazardly given promise to return and take her away from the small town of their youth. Perhaps if she had demanded to know what he truly felt about her at the time, and if she had searched her own heart, or if either of them had been given to more introspection, they might have understood more about their complicated feelings for each other. And that might have changed everything. But it had never happened, and neither of them had confessed any strong emotions to the other. She had always been afraid of his remoteness, afraid of what he might say if she pressed him too hard. It had begun that way and now, she thought, it would end that way. Theirs was a guarded and quiet relationship.

You could have a marriage like that, of course, she understood. It could even be a successful marriage. Expressions of deep affection weren't really necessary in a relationship like theirs, which was more based on comfortable habits. And except for that one day, neither of them had ever said or done anything other than what was expected. But this one time, he had revealed something profounder about himself than she had ever imagined. And this one thing, this surprising revelation, convinced her that what was unspoken between them was something precious and important, even if it would always, like a shadow, remain dark and obscure.

"Grace," Richard called from the living room. "Where's my drink? What's going on in there?"

"Just cleaning up a bit," she answered. "I'll be just a minute or two."

But she had no intention of hurrying. She wanted to enjoy the memory now that it had come back to surprise her. So many years ago, but still so vivid!

She remembered lying in the narrow hospital bed, propped up on the rough sheets and pillows, her face streaked with tears and flushed with livid blotches. She still had a terrible headache and parched mouth—the after-effects of the anesthesia. Even now she could recall the bitter taste of unconsciousness.

She could see no window because it was not even a room, just a small enclosed space around the bed and curtains that separated her from the other patients. Next to her was a chair and a small table with a water bottle and a glass straw. It seemed to her that she had been in this place once before. Surely, the misery of pain and despair were the same as before. And the failure haunted her too. The only conscious noise she remembered had been her own sobs, but they had finally ended, swallowed up in her exhaustion and pain. Nonetheless, the feeling of desperation had remained and deepened. When Richard, sitting by the bed, had tried to console her, reaching out to touch her hand, she turned away from him and buried her face in the pillow. She refused to look at him, knowing that he would be unable to disguise his disappointment. It had happened again! And he would blame her with unspoken recriminations that she would recognize even if he tried to master them with a forced smile.

She became suddenly aware that he had spoken, and of course, she heard him, but she hadn't quite understood. Maybe he was trying to console her. To her, words were just a stream of broken sounds without meaning. He seemed to realize it, and so he fell still for a long time and just watched her. Then, abruptly, he got up to leave. She moved her head to watch him, and for just a moment, she thought she saw something resolute and a slight stiffening of his back. He turned once, without a word, to look back at her, and then disappeared through a gap in the curtains. Even now she could remember the squeak of his shoes on the linoleum floor as he walked away.

So it had happened a second time, another stillbirth, with all the excitement and anticipation, and then the agony of labor, and finally the regret and shame that hollowed out a new and much deeper anguish. She had been so confident, and the doctor had assured her that the first time was unusual. She was healthy, young, energetic, and she had loved the baby that was growing inside her. She had felt it moving, pounding its little fists and kicking against the walls of its confinement, eager to conquer the world. But then, after a long, excruciating delivery, when she finally emerged from the black and timeless void of the anesthetic, she had looked through the gauze of her awakening to see the empty arms of the nurse.

She had been afraid to ask and just lay quietly, waiting to hear words that she dreaded.

"I'm very sorry, Dear. The doctor will explain," the nurse said finally.

"I don't want an explanation," she said, trying to shout above her weakness. But she did want to know: desperately. Was it a girl or boy? She wondered if that was some kind of morbid curiosity on her part. Would it deepen her despair to know? She had been prepared to say: "I'm so happy it's a boy, or I'm so happy it's a girl!" It wouldn't have mattered even if, without admitting it, she had wanted a girl. How could you not prefer one to the other?

One side of the curtain parted suddenly, thrust back by the doctor, who approached her bed. He placed a hand on her shoulder. It felt warm, but it made her shiver.

"I'm very sorry, Mrs. Collins, but your child was stillborn. We did everything we could, but the baby had already died before delivery. There was nothing to be done. Try to rest now."

She pulled herself up on her elbows and looked at him.

"Is it something I did?" she said. "This is the second time. I don't understand. Please. tell me."

"It's nothing you did. Very unusual, I admit. In fact I've never seen a case like yours before. It's just terribly unlucky."

"Does that mean it will happen again... if I tried."

"I don't think so," he said. "You can't blame yourself. Perhaps it was for the best."

"What do you mean?"

"Perhaps something was wrong with the child. It could be nature's way of sparing you some tragedy. I know that might seem cruel to say this, but..."

"And it was a girl wasn't it?" she said after a minute, because she knew.

"Yes."

"I was so sure!" She clenched her fists hard under the covers, trying not to cry again.

"We'll keep you for another day or two," the doctor said. "Just to make sure you recover properly."

He turned to leave.

She wanted to ask him, but couldn't say the words. Her breasts were tender and swollen and her nightgown had patches of wet—damp stigmata of her failure. She wanted to know when it would stop: this physical reminder of a dead baby that oozed out of her like a poison, but she couldn't bring herself to ask.

The nurse drew the curtains again, and she was alone.

Perhaps she slept a long while; she didn't know. There was no clock, and she had no watch, and there was no daylight or night to mark off time in the ward. But when she woke, she felt groggy, and her head was pounding as if several hours had passed. She sat up carefully and then slung her feet onto the cold floor. Leaning over, she found a pair of paper slippers and edged her feet into them. Standing, slowly, cautiously, she pulled the curtain aside and looked out into the room. There were several cubicles set off by curtains and visible in the glare of fluorescent ceiling fixtures. In the corner, sitting at a desk, was a nurse she did not recognize. She glanced up as Grace shuffled toward the door.

"I'll be back in a moment," she said.

"Yes, Dear," the nurse said. "And tell me if there's anything you need."

When she returned to her bed, she slept again, and only gradually awakened because she sensed the presence of someone sitting in the chair beside her.

When she opened her eyes, she could see that it was Richard. He reached over and touched her before he stood up.

"Are you fully awake?" he said.

"Yes, I suppose so," she mumbled.

"Then I'll call for the nurse."

He left through the parted curtain, and she could hear him say something so softly that she couldn't make it out, just liquid syllables dripping from his deep voice.

The curtain parted again, and he returned, followed by the nurse.

Grace sat up, her elbows digging into the bed, and stared, not quite believing what she saw.

"But I thought..." she began. "Is that my baby?"

"Yes," Richard said. "Your healthy baby boy!"

"But the doctor told me. I'm sure I heard right. And the nurse heard it too. I don't understand! A boy?"

"I couldn't let you suffer, Grace," he said. "I just couldn't. I had to do something. You were so sad. I've never seen anyone so sad and disappointed in my life."

"But then it's not mine then. Where did you—how did you get it? What have you done?"

"I pulled a few strings, Grace. It wasn't easy. I had to call in some favors: a colleague at the firm had a friend who had a friend. But it's done. You have a child."

She looked at his eager, smiling face and then at the nurse.

"But I don't want him," she said softly. "He's not mine. How could you do such a thing without asking me? Is it even legal?"

"It's done, Grace. I'm sure you'll grow to love him. He's just a wee thing now. And handsome. Take a close look."

The nurse stepped forward and said, "Don't you want to hold him? See him? He's a darling. Why, I see you have milk."

Grace pulled the sheet up around her neck.

"No. Take him away. He's not mine. I won't. I couldn't... ever."

"Please, Grace, be reasonable," Richard said.

"How can I be reasonable when you've done something so terrible without asking me? How could you?"

"It's all right," the nurse said. "I can put him with the

other babies in the Newborn Nursery until you're ready."

"I'll never be ready," Grace said. "And you, Richard, I don't know if I can ever forgive you for this."

"Honey, please!" he said, "I just couldn't let you suffer."

At that moment, she heard a very faint and muffled cry, nothing like what she had come to expect from a baby, but just a soft, weak whimper. Something inside her tightened and then released.

"All right," she almost shouted, on the verge of tears. "Come back. I'll just look before you take him away."

The nurse walked to the bed and gently lowered her bundle onto her breast, pulling the swaddling blanket aside.

The baby looked up at her, opened his eyes, and started to squirm, making two tight little fists.

"All right," she said, after several seconds. "Enough! Take him away. I don't...."

The nurse picked the baby up gently and left. Richard remained silent, staring at his wife. Finally, he said, "I know everything has been a shock for you. And now this second jolt. But I had to make it right. You were so desperate."

"Was it just for me?" she said. "Weren't you just as disappointed as I was? You did this for yourself, didn't you, not me?"

"That's not fair. And you're wrong. I did it for both of us. You'll see."

"And I suppose you can't take him back?"

"Grace, Grace! He's not like a used car. I've signed all the papers. Give him a chance. I know you'll come to love him."

She was quiet for a long time and then said finally: "If I have to, I suppose I can try. But maybe you'll regret this some day. Sometimes you are so rash, Richard! And selfish. And I can't bring myself to breast feed him. Don't expect that. It just wouldn't seem right."

"I guess I understand," he said, reaching out to grasp her hand.

She snatched it away and buried her face in the stiff pillow to muffle her sobs.

And yet now, she thought, sitting in the kitchen and staring at her wrinkled hands, knowing that he was waiting for her in the next room, this had been the most loving thing he had ever done, even if it had changed everything.

"What's going on in there?" Richard called out. "What are you doing?"

"Just a minute," she replied. But this once, she thought to herself, she wouldn't leap up at his insistence. She wanted to finish this memory. She needed to.

Having a newborn was just one alteration in their lives, but a catalyst for so many things that followed. For several days, they put off choosing a name, despite the insistence of the hospital staff. Grace, when she had to, was happy enough to refer to the baby as 'him.' But finally, however, Richard found a book of names and after rummaging through it, suggested 'Seth,' meaning the third son of Adam. According to the accompanying definition, the name meant a child that was a replacement. She had argued, at first, against this unorthodox choice, especially knowing its arcane meaning, because she feared it would always remind her of how he had entered their lives. But eventually, she agreed.

When the lying-in period at the hospital was over, and

Grace and the newborn returned to the little house on South Hoyne Avenue in the Beverly section of Chicago, it quickly became obvious that the circumstances were too cramped for all of them. Richard took to pacing around their small living room, avoiding the cluttered furniture, as if he was measuring off the space.

"We need to move," he declared one winter afternoon when Seth was about six months old. "This isn't a place to raise a child. A chain-link fence and a hard scrabble back yard for him to play in? And an alley filled with broken glass and overflowing trash cans? Where will he ride his bicycle and explore? Or learn to throw a baseball?"

"You mean, don't you, you want a place where you will play golf on Sundays?" Grace asked, not looking up from the book she was reading.

"I wasn't thinking just of myself, Grace."

"But you are part of the equation, aren't you?"

"No denials, I admit," he said. "I'd love to move out south where there's more space. In fact I've been doing some research and found just the small town for us. Not too far from Beverly, and it's on the Illinois Central so I can ride into the city every morning."

"And does it have a golf course?"

"Two, as a matter of fact. But that's just incidental."

"Of course it is." She had laughed about this because she realized that the move would be perfect for both of them.

The baby, Seth, was a tetchy infant, demanding and stubborn. His days were their nights—or rather Grace's nights, because Richard understood that a father's duty should revolve around discipline, instruction in sports—at least the ones he knew (largely golf and how to throw a baseball)—and the occasional and reluctant assistance to relieve his wife's exhaustion and impatience. In his mind there were very distinct duties of husband and wife, even if the rules remained unspoken. And, for that matter, he had been attracted to Grace, in part, because of her domestic suitability. Educated at the University of Chicago, with a home economics degree, she had come from a strange family, not unlike his own, in Southern Illinois. But one that made her perfect in his eyes.

She had told him her story in disjointed segments, but it eventually made him understand and cherish her.

Grace's mother had died young (she speculated it was from the overwork of tending to five children; one of them just an infant)—but it more probably was the flu that broke out in the United States after the war that killed her, making its lethal visits even to the remotest corners and obscure places like the little declining coal town where she grew up. Of course, it was the railroads and buses and airplanes that introduced the plague to that and every obscure corner of the country, carrying soldiers back from war, and spreading the deadly influenza to anyone weak or tired or just over-worked. And their house backed up across the back yard to a terminal span of turn-around tracks, as if the whistles, clangs, and snorts of steam engines were audible symbols of their connection to the perils traveling to them from the distant killing fields of Korea.

When her mother died, Grace, the oldest, became the surrogate in charge, while her father ignored the family as much as possible to pursue a life of whatever pleasures were on offer in a small, deteriorating coal mining town. Frugal in everything but his own pleasures, he expected an orderly household, disciplined by the virtues of his strict, but unpracticed Methodist faith. In an explosive and changing age when religion failed to regulate liquor or sin or greed, and when almost every other delight that was once proscribed was practiced in the breach, this tidy household, presided over by Grace, was both aware of the changing morals of the outside world, but strict, by necessity, in its interior discipline. So Grace grew up quickly, skipping over the uncertain years of adolescence and entering into adulthood with the sudden change in the family's fortune.

If this situation imparted any lessons to her, it was the value of self-control and self-sacrifice. While the rest of the country was acquiring new habits of indulgence, "home made" and "home grown" still seemed infinitely better than "store bought," even if the task imposed upon her in preparing meals was onerous. "Making do" became an often-voiced and always-respected mantra to be invoked at every encounter with a sparse cupboard, and second only to the concept of "stretching" which meant making do with the same shortage. And later, when she was much older and married, Grace, although living in considerable luxury, imposed shortages and limitations on her sons for the sake of remembering her childhood. It was too much a part of her personality to rescind old habits of frugality. Perhaps this translation of the meager opportunities of her adolescence to her children would have seemed cruel in the absence of its necessity, but her kindness and unyielding values made it seem to be a mere eccentricity. Who could argue with her? And Richard had often teased her about it in good humor.

Despite his absent and distant manner, Grace's father

had imparted one virtue to all his children: and that was a respect for education. Whether consciously or not, he was just passing along the tradition from a long lineage of school teacher aunts and uncles—a family tree of modest but dedicated learners. Ironically, though, his admiration for learning and, specifically, for a college degree proved to be an escape hatch through which all five siblings would eventually pass. The only praise he ever distributed to his sons and daughters was for their academic excellence. All else he considered to be vanity.

The result of this odd combination of strict morals and educational ambition was five earned higher degrees: the two brothers passed through medical school, two sisters became English teachers after four years at an Illinois normal college, and, of course, there was Grace, with her Chicago degree in economics. To say in general what this family accomplished, it was a service of social correction: the two doctors who imposed discipline on the body and the English teachers who struggled to correct and enlighten the crude expressions of their wayward students. If Grace differed slightly from this curriculum, never actually working except part time before she met Richard, she made up for it in her upright demeanor and moral sensitivity, which she tried to apply to her new child, Seth, and later, to her other two sons. Inevitably, almost, her extended family of brothers and sisters had dispersed, and the poverty that had once bound them together dissipated with their successes. She only thought of them now because life had seemed to move in a circle and she had become, once again, the custodian of her family and now of her gravely ill husband.

"Are you OK in there? What's the matter" Richard called to her.

"Fine, just fine," she replied. "I'm straightening up in the kitchen. I'll be with you in a second."

But she made no move to get up. Something made her want to continue these memories—the story of her life entwined with his that had become so important and would be even more critical when her sons arrived.

What had been the strangest consequence, she remembered, and unexpected after her two desperate stillbirths and the fateful adoption of Seth, had been the live birth of two more sons, spaced evenly apart by four years, so that the distribution of children matched three familiar childhood cycles. It was as if this strange, unwanted adopted boy, this interloper scooped out of another woman's womb and placed in her arms, had cured whatever ailed her, and she could now successfully bear her own children.

The first of these "legitimate" (because she was sure that Seth had been born from some illicit union), was named Dexter (Deck for short), a name meaning right-handed like everyone in her family. Indeed, Seth, from the beginning, had favored his left as if to confirm that he would always be at odds with the rest of them. And the two brothers were as different as their heritage might have indicated. While Seth was stocky and out-going, crawling at an early age and constantly clumsy in his terrestrial wanderings, knocking over anything left in his path like an enthusiastic puppy, Deck, on the other hand, just seemed content to observe and judge everything, as if a child could measure his surroundings and estimate their value. The third son, arriving four years later, was named Nick, Nicholas—from an obscure mention in the Bible, but more likely named for one of Grace's brothers. He was a child entirely wrapped up in himself, always with an amused, but distracted look on his face and exploding with the sounds of imaginary musical instruments.

"Damn it, Grace," Richard called from the living room. "Am I getting that drink tonight or whenever?"

"Hold on. I'm coming," she said.

Grace shook the memories from her mind and stood up. She poured two fingers of whiskey over an ice cube into his glass and then splashed a smaller amount into hers. Standing up, she made her way back into the living room and set the drinks on the table. She sat down in the chair that made the right angle to the couch where he was sitting.

"What took you so long?" he asked abruptly.

"I don't know. Just remembering things."

"Something I did?"

"Never mind," she said. "It's not important." But she thought that these were the most important memories she possessed, even if she had no intention of mentioning them to him now. He would never completely understand, no matter how many times they had talked about their children, nor how much about how the gift of the baby, Seth, had changed their lives around. After all these years, there were still a great many things that she couldn't share with him, and now there wasn't time anymore.

CHAPTER 3

Deck raised his body carefully on one elbow so he wouldn't jostle her. He peered across the bed at her still body—to see if she was still asleep. He knew she liked it when he looked over at her, stretched out next to him with her eyes closed. This morning, he thought, she was probably aware, in her feigned drowsiness, of his admiration. He was tempted to reach over and pull aside the mass of brown curls that covered one side of her face. But that would break the spell, and she would turn toward him, and he wanted to linger in the moment.

He looked away and stared up at the ceiling, thinking perhaps that he too might sleep a few minutes more before their long day began. But his anticipation prodded him wide awake, and his heart began to race almost as if he had been running. For no good reason that he could think of, this tightening in his chest always occurred when he contemplated a trip to Southern Illinois to visit his parents. And today would be just that much worse. He knew that his father had been ill for some time, although what it was, exactly, was never explicitly described in their phone calls or email messages. His parents were adept at hiding things, and especially now, as if the disease and condition of his father was somehow shameful. Or maybe it was just that he could never confess to any weakness.

It made him wonder if clumsiness and misunderstanding were always the true condition between fathers and sons: and if the inevitable shifting relation of one generation to another was always fraught and angry because of what was simultaneously being lost and what was gained—the substitution, the challenge, the rise and decline. Perhaps it was not anger, but his reluctance. Just terribly reluctant to show affection. That was his father! There ought to be some sort of ceremony, he thought, something formal about such transitions in the way he imagined had once existed. He was sure he read about something like that somewhere, some ritual where the father ceded to the son. He seemed to have a vague memory of it. Some society—something historic: The father dispatched on a canoe down the rapids when his strength was failing.

He almost laughed out loud about that. He could just imagine the scene—shoving his father off across the lake in a rowboat!

But maybe that was exactly the purpose of this family reunion. Was it to be some commemoration of passing? And if so, that would be doubly—no triply—stressful because the power or whatever mysterious energy there was to be handed down from his father (if that was his intention) would be dispersed, not just to him, but also divided with his two other brothers. His brothers!

"And there's a weird bunch," he said under his breath. Nick and Seth: especially Seth. And with his mother nervously hovering over all of them, clucking her worries! He wondered how much he should tell his sleeping partner about them—warn her about his family before she encountered them. She would be curious, of course, partly because the invitation to accompany him had come late, and they hadn't much time to discuss it. And she would ask him, no doubt, why he wanted her to be included. But at the same time, she might assume that an introduction to his parents meant something significant and deepening about their own relationship—suggesting some permanent attachment. He wanted her to be there, as much as anything as a distraction. But he had to be careful. Yes, he would have to be very careful not to let something merely convenient become a commitment he couldn't extricate himself from.

He had casually said to her: "I'm going to a family reunion; perhaps you'd like to come with me. Odd family; my parents and two brothers, but it's a nice setting. You'll really like the house and the lake."

She had readily agreed, perhaps too enthusiastically, and that worried him.

Recently, he had been trying to understand the reasons for his reluctance to face his parents alone. If he was honest with himself, it had always made him uneasy to visit them. But more so lately, and he had now taken to bringing along a companion to the house on the lake—at least since his father had retired. He was certain that his parents' constant intimacy, and living mostly by themselves, had changed them and made them strangers to him. He wondered what it would be like to be isolated and aging: how it might trap them in an envelope of unthinking rituals and words and ideas expressed in a language of their own loneliness. He had noticed that they spoke less to him in their phone conversations, only repeating the same questions and answering in the same vague ways.

And sometimes it seemed that their words were intended just for themselves: thoughts and complaints escaping in an unedited, single monologue. As if in a room alone together. And with him the unseen observer.

It always seemed worse when one or both of his brothers were present, perhaps because they had never invented a secret code among themselves. Maybe that was it. They had no repertoire of gestures—no knowing glances to share an emotion, no silent form of communication with which they could convey their shared impatience or exasperation. He often wondered why they hadn't grown up to invent their own underground society in an alliance against their parents, in the way he imagined other siblings had done. It wasn't normal, he thought, for brothers to be so distant from each other, and so different in temperament that they had failed to invent a special relationship that was unintelligible and opaque to their parents—a unique dialect of shrugs, nods, and facial expressions to share their feelings. At least that was something he had seen his friends do. Maybe it was because their parents treated all of them so differently that they became oddly *unfamilial*. (Was that even a word, he wondered?) If not, there should be one to describe this odd clan he had been born into.

And now, when he needed someone to reflect his thoughts, he had to import a confidant for those moments when, instead of a sigh or a sharp word, he could just change his expression and that person would know—someone to whom he could signal his annoyance or frustration. So he would need to school her to her temporary duty, and describe his family so that she would understand why she had been invited.

What the hell, he thought. *You could really over-analyze everything. And it's just like me to make a bad situation worse.* What he did know for sure was that he didn't want to go, and he didn't want to see his brothers, and he was afraid of what his father was going to announce.

She stirred slightly, and put her hand lightly on his thigh, and he turned toward her again.

"Awake finally?" he asked.

"Almost," she sighed.

"Then I think we should get up. It's a long drive—a long day."

"Just one minute more. Isn't it awfully early?" she said, moving her hand slightly. "It's not even light yet. What time is it?"

He grasped her fingers in his hand and then sat up abruptly. Swinging his feet onto the floor, he turned back to her.

"You don't want to know. But we've got to get going," he said. "It's a long drive."

"Yeah, so you said," she sighed, frowning slightly.

After a quick breakfast, they loaded his car with their luggage and joined the early morning stream of traffic leaving the city. They emerged quickly from the dense, dark canyons of Chicago and then passed by the monotonous outskirts of the city, where one identical appendage of gas stations and fast-food joints after another of the suburbs reached out to touch the edge of the Interstate highway. It wouldn't be before they reached the middle of the state that the endless carpet of corn and soybean fields would stretch out in front and to the sides of them in the noonday sun. On other trips, he had been tempted to set his GPS on some sort of alternate, slower route when he made this drive, something that would take him along narrow roads through small towns and past farmhouses, slowing sometimes behind a dawdling tractor. But for a reason he well understood, he felt rushed and anxious to get to that place and the rendezvous he dreaded.

"So what are they like?" she asked, turning toward him.

"My brothers? Or my parents?"

"All of them."

"Well, Susan, they're hard to describe, but I'll try," he said, glancing quickly at her and then back. At other times he might have preferred to watch her reaction as he described the family. But there was also something satisfying about concentrating on the road in front of him and allowing his consciousness to wander aimlessly through his memories and impressions of them, saying what first came to mind, as if there were no audience other than his own recollections. Somehow this seemed to be more like the unguarded and honest truth. And he would not have to watch the impression his words made on her or allow her to interrupt.

"My dad. I guess I should begin there," he said. "He was a lawyer in a big firm downtown. Made partner when he was very young. He took me to the office once or twice, down in the Loop. It was all old dark wood, thick rugs, and hush-hush: walk softly and don't speak.

"You know, it's funny now that I think about it, but he was, and still is, a guy who was always an attorney, even around the house. What I mean is that he was always judging us, as if we had signed some sort of contract that laid out strict rules of behavior—or maybe a kind of promissory note of expectations. I don't think he could help it—he couldn't turn it off. I think I was afraid of him for a long time, and then—I don't know, I just decided I'd never get to know him. He wasn't mean or anything. Just distant and abrupt.

"I'm pretty sure he wanted me to follow in his footsteps; he never said it in so many words, but I felt the pressure. But I couldn't. I'd seen too much, and I never wanted to be like him. I always got the feeling from him that legal matters existed like some sort of exalted moral realm where, you know, the gods of righteousness battled against wrong, and where blind justice would always triumph. I could never understand how anything so abstract and boring could be something you could commit your life to. So I think he decided that I had failed him."

"That sounds awful," she interrupted.

"It wasn't. Not really," he continued, "because it allowed me to be myself. You'll probably wonder why I feel this so strongly, because I'm sure you'll find him charming and outgoing—good with strangers and a pleasant, friendly man. And he is. But he was just never that way with us. I've thought about this a lot, and I decided that there are some guys who should never have children, perhaps because they, themselves, never really had much of a childhood. Born already an adult. Odd thing to say, but.... Can't blame him, really though. 'Cause he grew up without his own father, who died way back when, and I suppose he just never learned how to act like one. It wasn't that he was overly strict, but he was never really there, not all of him at least, like he was always thinking about something else. Something that was more important. So when he spoke to us, it was like hearing a pronouncement of some weird oracle who happened, just by some accident, to be standing in your living room. Everything he said was firm and decisive, and I doubt he ever questioned himself—at least I never heard any doubts. And the worst part—you're going to think I'm odd when I say this—but the worst part is that I don't think he ever touched me, out of affection or out of anger, either. He expected to be obeyed, to accept his advice, even when we didn't want it, even when we resisted, and I'll tell you, even though I knew he meant well. But he just wasn't much of a physical presence except when he was."

Susan put her hand on his shoulder and squeezed gently.

He paused, realizing that he was gripping the steering wheel too firmly. "Damn it, no!" he said. "No, I don't really mean anything the way it sounds. You're going to think I rehearsed all this, but I've thought a lot about him. You see, he was there, obviously, but I never got the impression that he could actually see me. And I certainly never knew him the way Mom did, or maybe his law partners. Oh, of course, there were funny stories he told about himself every once in a while, but they could have just as easily been about anyone: *Anonymous Tales of an Unknown Author*. And he had a lot of friends. But what he felt inside was buried a fathom too deep to be visible to us. If you can imagine it, he was a man who held his emotions close in."

"Oh, Deck, I'm surprised you survived," she said suddenly, "you make it sound so awful."

"Yeah, except that it really wasn't so bad," he said, as if he was still trying to convince himself. "Because it meant that I was ignored, and I could become whatever or whoever I wanted, and I guess he thought that was OK, even when he disapproved of my choices and wasn't afraid to tell me so. But he left me alone most of the time. Not my mother, of course. But that's another story. And also lucky that I wasn't either of my brothers."

"I really don't understand now," she said. "You're confusing me, Deck."

"Well, there's Nick and Seth. And they are very different, and he acted completely different with each of them. To each his own!"

He drove on, distracted for a minute by a sudden clot of slow traffic stuck behind two trucks, one crawling at a slow pass around the other. When it cleared, he continued:

"I guess the way he never paid any attention to me made me determined to catch his attention."

"So that's why you went into finance or whatever you do? You've been vague about it, Deck. You haven't really told me."

"All I can say is that it didn't work. He didn't seem to care very much, no matter what I accomplished, or at least he never said he approved. But I think he was really disappointed. If I wasn't going to be a lawyer—his first and great love—then I suppose it didn't matter. Although some times I suspected he might have been proud of me, just for standing up to him."

He glanced over at her. She had turned to stare out the window, although there was nothing much to see except a line of cars in front and a weary landscape. He didn't want to tell her, however, that his mother often pestered him about his marriage plans. His non-existent marriage plans. And every time he mentioned someone or when he brought a companion to the house, her eyes became bright with enthusiasm, and she always managed to catch him by himself and ask him if this was the one:

"Is Bea or Marilyn the one?" she had asked, "or Cindy?"

It had stopped troubling him to see her disappointment

when he just shrugged and said, "We'll see." Knowing, of course, that he could never imagine himself caught in the predicament of anything permanent.

He hadn't sorted out his feelings very well when he thought about why he was determined to remain single, except that it seemed as strong as any commitment could be. Maybe it came from being a member of such a strange family: so outwardly normal, but inside, so fraught with tension and—worst of all—those extended silences of disapproval and looks of disappointment. There were moments when he feared that he might carry some genetic defect that prevented a long-term commitment. Maybe, he thought, there was something inside him: some trace he inherited from his parents that would condemn any permanent relationship of his to repeat the way they mixed and confused unhappiness and love. Yeah, fucked up DNA. For sure, dynasty was destiny. But was their clan so different, really? Was his family so strange, so unlike others?

One thing he did know, and maybe that had made all the difference, was the constant irritant in all their lives: his brother Seth. His adopted brother Seth: the cuckoo in the nest, the splinter under everyone's skin. But maybe he was just kidding himself. It was probably partly his own fault that he was distant from his older brother.

But maybe the reality was that he just enjoyed being single because, almost by instinct, he had learned that relationships could tear you down and strip you bare until you were nothing but an appendage of someone else's needs. At least that was what he thought he had learned from his family. But especially, there was always Seth, the trouble maker.

In spite of these morose explorations triggered by his

anxious anticipation of the coming reunion, he did love his family, deeply and permanently. And the wounds he probed were—none of them—mortal. He just didn't know what he thought. And he surely shouldn't confuse Susan any more.

So he knew he couldn't really explain any of this to her, because he couldn't articulate what it meant to himself. She would never understand. It was a conflict he had learned to live with, perhaps of his own making.

"What about your mother, then?" she asked, slipping a hand behind his neck and rubbing gently.

Almost as a reflex, he took his foot off the accelerator.

"Why don't we stop and have a coffee," he said. "It's really hard for me to concentrate on the road and talk to you about my parents at the same time. I start remembering too much and, well, it's distracting."

"Sure," she said, removing her hand.

They drove on in silence for twenty more minutes until the next exit.

"Junk food and junk motels," he said as they passed by the sign that announced "Food and Lodging, This Exit."

"Doesn't matter. Coffee is coffee and I'm ready to stop. What's the hurry?"

He chose a booth at the back of the noisy restaurant. They sat, facing each other, two paper mugs and several torn sugar envelopes scattered on the table.

"It's still a couple of hours before we get there," he said. "Are you tired?"

"Not really," she said. "But still curious about you and your family, and about why the stories you tell about them are so complicated."

"Just as a kind of warning, I suppose."

"Because I might say the wrong thing?"

"No, because *they're* sure to say the wrong thing, and I don't want you to be surprised or offended."

"That's not very encouraging. You keep sounding like you don't like them."

"I'm not sure I do. But you don't get to choose your parents, do you?"

"Maybe you deserve them," she said.

He looked at her and laughed. "I like that; I really like that. Yes, I suppose we deserve the parents we get, even if it's only from a chance coupling of two strands of chromosomes. Yeah, probably."

"So tell me about your mother. What's she like? After what you've told me about your father, I'm curious about who would marry someone like that—and stay."

"All emotion and sentiment," he said. "Let me put it this way: I know it's a crazy example, but you'll get it. So, if you've ever seen one of those television courtroom dramas where a witness begins to stray off the point, and they start to relate something really complicated, embroidered with detail, and then the judge looks stern and leans over the podium and says, 'Will the witness just answer the question?' Well, that's her. If my dad never understood how to be a father, she could be a mother twice-over.

"You know, my old-fashioned dad could still imagine that his only duty as a father was disciplinarian-in-chief with a side obligation to instruct us in sports—at least the couple he knew. But I never saw him pick up a dirty dish or help her in the kitchen. I'm sure in his mind there are very distinct duties of husband and wife, even if I never actually heard him say that outright. But I think he must have chosen her—Grace is her name—because of her suitability. It's amazing to think about it, but she was actually educated at the University of Chicago with an economics degree way back when. And she was from a strange family, not very different from his own, in Southern Illinois, although weird in a different way. But one that made her perfect in his eyes. Despite her education, I guess he always pictured her in an apron."

"You make that place they come from sound pretty backward," she said. "Is everyone like that?"

"Yes, I suppose. Something in the air or the soil that pollutes the water and makes everyone grow up with some part of them stunted."

She thought to herself, *like you?* But remained silent: *No joking with this guy when he is on a tear.*

"My Mom? I think you'll like her. All tradition, even though she had a good education. I guess from having so many brothers and sisters and being the oldest, and having a bastard for a father—I never really knew him very well. Sort of brought them up. Anyway, I guess she learned how to run interference from growing up that way. I think she considered it her duty to stand up to Dad when he started in on us. Forever making excuses for us, especially Seth, who was always teetering on the edge of trouble. She had two brothers and two sisters—my uncles and aunts. I knew them all when I was much younger, but I don't think they're very close any more—at least the brother and sister who are still alive. One of them lives in Seattle and the other in New York somewhere. You know, it's strange, but you remind me of her somehow...."

"So I imagine that Mom was really anxious to get out of that small town, and Chicago was a great place to be. That's where she met my father. They've never told me how or where, and I don't think either of them is very romantic about it. He's sure not the type to reminisce! Anyway, my dad got this big job as a partner in a law firm in Chicago. By the time I was born, they had moved, with my older brother, Seth, to a suburb on the south side. And that's where I grew up. My mom never did have a job, although I think she surely could have. Maybe wanted to."

"I'd be very frustrated," Susan interrupted. "I mean if you have an education and not doing something with it. But maybe things were different back then."

"Well, it's not so long ago, but I suppose she was pretty occupied with us. You can understand that because we were all born four years apart, and that makes eleven or twelve years of cleaning bottoms and pushing pabulum into fussy mouths. With no help from the coach on the sidelines. It had to be difficult, and the irony of it is that she seemed destined to repeat that strange childhood-adulthood of hers with us."

"It's hard for me to imagine her," Susan said. "I mean what she looks like."

"Well, I think it's pretty hard to describe your own mother because you've seen her in so many different ways. But I'd say, from pictures I've seen at least, that she was really beautiful once, but in a kind of upright and tight-wound way. It's difficult for me to explain what I mean, but, well, maybe it's just the pose she struck when she was being photographed, but there's something rigid about her, as if relaxing would bring on chaos. Maybe she stands too straight and holds herself too self-consciously. I don't know."

"Is she like that now?"

"Not really. No. It's just what I remember from earlier.

I think you'll see that she's pretty ordinary and pleasant too. But the two of them together, well. You're prepared."

"I guess I am, but a bit anxious, too."

She didn't add that she was sure Deck was exaggerating—the way some guys she knew loved to talk tragedy about their families, almost bragging about surviving terrible circumstances. It made them sound like the heroes of their childhood.

"But don't worry, Susan. You'll really like the house they live in, and the lake is beautiful, although I guess it's ironic that they ended up in the part of Illinois that both of them had fled from. Anyway. And you can just ignore my brothers. I try to."

She didn't respond, but reached over and put her hand on his arm, just for a minute, to reassure him. But she was thinking that this might be the severest trial she would have to face with him, and if she passed through it without a major mistake, then perhaps this might have serious consequences for her... for their future together.

She took a sip of her coffee—cold and bitter by now—and looked anxiously at him, but he made no sign he was ready to leave yet. She didn't want to tell him how bored and uncomfortable she had been listening to the intimate tales about his family. Exaggerations, no doubt. And on and on; it sounded rehearsed, somehow.

In the time she had known him, he had never once talked about his family. And now, there was this sudden overload of information about them. But she suspected that any family was only interesting to its members, and certainly his had a closed circle of appeal. God, she thought, anything but a conversation about genealogy if that was coming next! And how was she supposed to react to what he had told her? Empathy? Forewarned? It was just a confusing muddle of details that she'd never remember anyway, even if she wanted to. It made her wonder why he had brought her along, and what role she was supposed to play.

"Shouldn't we get back on the road now?" she asked.

"No. Not yet. There's just a bit more you need to know: about my brothers."

She said nothing, but thought: *Oh my God! There's more?*

"There's Nick," he said. "Professional cello player, sort of. Four years younger than me and unmarried. He never says much, and certainly doesn't reveal anything about his life. Could be gay; in fact, I'm certain he is. Pretty obvious, but never came out to the family. Can't blame him for that. You'd never know how they'd react. Bit of a wimp. There's always a hole in what he tells you—some missing piece to the puzzle.

"And then there's Seth and his wife, Lee (she's Asian from somewhere out there), but mainly it's Seth you need to know about. He's my older brother—adopted, which explains a lot. I don't know where they found him, but he's always disrupting everything. I guess I sometimes admire him because he doesn't seem to take any family nonsense seriously, at least the way I do. It must seem irrelevant to him, his being a kind of outsider. Always makes my dad furious because everything he ever tried to do he's failed at, at least in their eyes. But I'll bet you'll like him. A big fellow who walks into a room and just takes over the conversation whether you like it or not. He's like a kid that way: demanding your attention and won't let you alone. Pesters you just to get your attention. Full of wild stories that make my dad furious.

"And you should see the two of them—my dad and him—go at it. They always do. Anything Seth says, my dad has to disagree with. It's like some kind of crazy singles match... tennis. Seth serves an exaggeration and Dad slams a correction right back at him. Deuce!! Makes everyone listening in tense as hell. And Seth just gets wilder and wilder, and Dad more and more stern. But you'll see. It's like a game of smash up volleys, and they can't help themselves."

"You make everyone sound so terrible, Deck! And I'm so confused about all of them. But please tell me I didn't sign up for a family free-for-all."

"Oh, you'll be OK because there's always me," he said. "You can always depend on me."

She wondered if that was true, or if she would just be an appalled bystander or a witness to something disturbing if it came to that. And she was beginning to wonder why she had agreed to this voyage. Except, of course, that she knew.

"All right," he said, finally standing up. "Let's go. Only a couple of hours from here. I'm sure you'll like the house. Beautiful sunsets across the lake."

"So you said. Well, at least there's that," she added.

Once they were under way again, neither of them uttered another word, and the tense silence between them convinced Deck that he had said far too much. It was too often this way: he was forever a teller of woe! He knew he suffered from a compulsion to puff up the disagreeableness of his family, but sometimes he couldn't help himself. Was it a way of bragging about his success, he wondered—how he escaped from them and made his own way? Or was it like the opening pages of some bad novel, setting a scene for the unfortunate hero who has to claw his way to inevitable good fortune? Even worse, should he admit it, the stories he had told her were incomplete—untrue because of their prejudiced angle. Yes, his family was strange, but he wondered if they were really so unusual. Because, in addition to the brief, almost gleeful account of their awfulness, there was much he had left unsaid that was real and tangible and almost funny that had made it possible for them all to survive. He had survived, at any rate—more than that; he had prospered. But how could he ever explain anything so complicated to her? And he certainly hadn't been honest about himself. He wondered if he should tell her that. Maybe his long discussion of his family was just a deflection. But what did he owe her anyway? He wasn't sure.

CHAPTER 4

Nick sat on the edge of his bed, pulling on his socks. Spread over the covers were several neat piles of clothes that he intended to pack into his suitcase. He could have hitched a ride with Deck, but neither of them had mentioned it when they last spoke, even though it would only be a short detour to pick him up in the small college town in Central Illinois where he taught music. But, he didn't want to spend any more time than he had to with his older brother and whatever woman he had tagging along. It frustrated him trying to keep up with his brother's revolving relationships, especially because they seemed more like a compulsion than a commitment, and he had trouble keeping track of their names. So, instead, he planned to take the bus over to Champaign and then catch the Amtrak down south. He could have driven, but he knew in that case that he'd have to bring his cello along, and his mother would pounce on him like a zealous fan, pleading for him to play something for the assembled family, and he just couldn't—not this time. Besides, this was certainly not the occasion for a concert. His father's condition, whatever it was, would transform any music into a dirge no matter what the verdict on his heath that he was about to announce. And he suspected the worst. And besides, the voice of a cello, particularly when played solo, sounded with such distressing indwelling sadness, and, almost always, a resonance of lamentation. No matter how joyous the piece he selected, there would always be something melancholic about the melody it expressed. That was one reason he loved the instrument; it suited him. But not for this occasion.

And worse, if he played for them, he was sure it would remind everyone of his miscarried career. Someone—Deck probably—would ask him how things were at the University—emphasizing *University*—and he'd have to remind them that he was still employed by the small community college at the wrong end of town, and not the campus on the hill. His brother always asked a question that sounded like an answer—meant to convey some tidbit of over-analysis, as if he was the family shrink and tasked with scrutinizing everyone's motivations and pointing out their shortcomings. He was his father's son.

And then Nick would have to explain, once again, to everyone that no, he was not even an adjunct member of the faculty of that fine music school located on the north side of town. He was only the stringed instrument instructor for the few students who didn't opt to play trombone for the marching band at his obscure and second-rate academy. Deck with all his fucking money! Deck from Chicago! Just pounding his chest and showing off his success like some financial Tarzan.

He didn't need to rush because he had plenty of time to get to the station. The only good thing about living next to the community college was its location near the Greyhound Terminal, and he could walk. One small advantage in his small life, he thought. Well, there was one other good thing: Mark. He'd have time to call, and Mark would be sympathetic. Maybe that was his friend's greatest attraction: understanding. No, he corrected himself, that wasn't it at all: there was way much more to their relationship than sympathy. Even though he was feeling anxious, it was, after all, just a family reunion and no need to bother his friend.

He almost had to laugh at the thought: imagining the family together. But the scene was inevitable: after everyone had said a sentence or two of hello, and when all the how-are-you's had been asked and answered, then they would gradually fall back into their old habits, squeezed into familiar niches as if no time whatsoever had passed, and they were still trapped into playing the same roles, and nothing had changed, and no one had grown up. But they couldn't change that regression any more than they would think to arrange themselves in different places at the table. Family, he thought, was the very definition of who you really were. No getting around it: the past always grabbed onto you and pulled you back in time, whenever you were together, back to who you had once been and would always be. Family refused to let you change—to become someone different. Damn it: no matter how you tried! That writer: someone like Sherwood Anderson or Thomas Wolfe—he wasn't sure—had said *you can't go home again.* But that was certainly wrong. In fact it was the opposite, because you couldn't ever really escape from whom you had been. Once he had hoped his family might be a refuge for his failures and grief—just some place where you were accepted as you always had been—unchanged.

But it could also be your own private corner of hell if you let it. What a cliché! He decided he'd call Mark anyway.

He picked up his cellphone and tapped on the FaceTime app. Mark answered almost immediately, and Nick could see that he was sitting in his kitchen with a small espresso cup on the table in front of him.

"On your way?" he asked.

"Yes. The Sirens are chanting, and I forgot to plug my ears."

"Will it be that bad?"

"Probably. Yeah. I'm about to wreck my ship trying to steer clear of all the family shoals."

"Well, at least you can still laugh about it."

"Yes. From a distance."

"I wish you'd let me go with you, Nick. For moral support. And, if you're shy about us, well, they have to know by now."

"Sure, they know. That's not my worry or their problem. It's the job. My career. I've explained as much as a million times it seems. And my dad always gives me a strange look whenever the subject of music comes up, like he believes it's some weird hobby of mine and not a real occupation. Like it was some sort of inadequacy that explains everything else about me. And, for sure, I'd be a better person if I did something else. Anything. Yeah. But they've known about me since I was a kid—probably even before I did. But no, I just wouldn't expose you to what's going to happen. This won't be a happy occasion. My father is really ill, and I don't know what else is going on. I like you too much to subject you to that. And there are my two brothers to boot."

"In sickness and health, don't you think?"

"No, I don't. I never took that idea seriously. Sickness changes everything."

"Well, good luck then. And call me if things get too difficult."

"You won't want to know."

"But I do. Really. Promise?"

"Okay. Deal."

"And one more thing, Nick: try not to get upset. Just let it happen—like you're watching some TV show—like Dr. Phil or an afternoon soap or Oprah."

"Now there's a thought."

He hung up and stared down at the darkening screen. He placed the cellphone on the bed and then stood up. Looking down, he was reminded of Seth. Damn him, why was he so obstinate. Refusing ever to get a cellphone. Probably some restriction or other of that weird religion of his, but he didn't want to know. The worst thing you could do was ask him something—any off-handed remark like *why don't you ever use a cellphone, Seth?* and he'd be sure to bring up something about his new faith. And that would turn on a sermon, and you'd learn all the things you weren't supposed to believe in—like evolution. Yes, he remembered.

He glanced around the room. Where was it: that pamphlet that Seth had sent a couple of months ago explaining the fundamentals of Creationism? And who knows what else? He had started to read it and then just tossed it aside. It was too crazy. Dinosaurs cavorting with cavemen. He didn't want to know how deeply his brother had descended into nonsense.

When he learned more about it, he wondered how Seth had found this profoundly strange devotion. It certainly wasn't a family inheritance. His parents were strictly

Easter Sunday and Christmas Eve Christians as far back as he could remember. He had always thought that their limited practice, such as it was, had been some kind of political statement, mainly for his father's benefit, so that he would be seen as a practical religious man who didn't let faith interfere with his judgement and a man who wouldn't allow emotion to clutter up his legal mind. But, also to be seen as someone who would be a responsible member of the community. What a careful and exacting person he had always been! But Seth. Wow! The exact opposite!

Seth, he thought, he hadn't seen him since their last reunion, whenever that was, but he was forever on his mind, like an irritating melody he couldn't forget. Seth, the errant brother! He was eight years older than Nick, but he knew that age could never account for their differences.

Almost as long as he remembered, he had wondered why his older brother was so peculiar, until he once overheard his parents talking:

"Oh, you know Seth. He never seems to fit in. Probably acting that way because he's adopted," his father had said.

He was still very young when he overheard these words, and he didn't quite know what they meant at the time, except that it sounded like some kind of failure. Thereafter, whenever the difference struck him, or when his brother acted in some odd fashion, he would repeat to himself, "Oh, he's adopted," even though the meaning was a puzzle. Eventually, he worked up the courage to ask his mother to explain the mystery of those unfamiliar words, because he was afraid that they meant something terrible. But he was curious and couldn't help himself.

"Seth is your brother," she said. "We chose him. That's what it means. And he's part of our family now, just like you and Deck are."

"But I don't understand?" he had insisted. "Why is he so different? What does that word mean?"

"It means a child who had to be given away. And we took him in."

"But why would someone give him away? I still don't understand, Mom. Didn't they want him?"

"No. They probably couldn't keep him. But we could, you see. We wanted him and made him part of our family. And you must never say anything about it. You have to promise me you won't. Especially to him."

"Sure," he had said. But that didn't stop him from wanting to know more.

Nick had sometimes been tempted to ask again, but he would imagine from his mother's determined expression that she would say nothing more. So he had to be satisfied with an explanation that was no explanation at all: only the instruction that he should never bring up the subject again.

He walked around the bed reaching for the piles of clothing he had laid out to place into his suitcase. He was tempted to pick up his cellphone and call Mark again, but he wasn't sure what he wanted to say. And he'd probably just fumble around searching to find some reason for another call. And he'd say a lot of stupid things. Of course, Mark would understand, and after a few more words they'd hang up. But he didn't.

Damn, he thought, *I really don't want to see my brothers again. Not when Dad is sick and dying maybe.* Just a lot of worries that he couldn't disentangle from thinking about encountering them all again under this cloud of apprehension.

But Seth! Of course, he eventually heard the whole story of his mother's failed pregnancies and her desperation. But it remained a confusing explanation that, once he knew, would often make him ponder. In fact, he was fascinated by Seth, especially when he was older and could ask himself how his brother, growing up in his family, with the same mother and father, could be so peculiar and remain such an outsider. It was as if his brother was immune to any effects of his environment. Nick sometimes admired him for this emotional solitude, and he envied his independence from the guilt he felt at his father's obvious disappointment in himself. And Seth also seemed unmoved by the jealousy that really bothered him when he came to realize that both parents seemed to favor Deck: Deck would be the success; Deck the chosen son. Maybe because of this, he sometimes considered Seth to be an ally—Seth who was able to break away. Except that he was entirely indifferent to taking sides.

He knew his parents made every effort to press their adopted son into the mold of their ambitions for him. He knew, because both parents confided in him and Deck, as if speaking their concerns out loud and sharing their worries would somehow evoke an explanation. He realized now that these conversations made things even stranger.

Of course, Seth resisted their best efforts—perhaps not consciously—who knew? But persistently. Where they wanted success for him, he always failed, at least in their eyes. And Nick heard stories that when he was quite young, only his father's upright reputation rescued him from a number of minor delinquencies. Yes, there was that.

And later, every effort to push him into higher education failed because Seth was just vague and seemed lost even in the small college that finally admitted him. So his parents had had to accept that he failed again. Nick wondered if they ever took responsibility for his behavior. And yet, he always thought that Seth was a happy, kind, and generous person. It was as if he grew up belonging to another clan, an exile living in the wrong tribe, but someone who never resented his situation or reacted to his parent's superior airs.

And yet, when he thought about his own life, he wondered if Seth really was actually the failure in the family. At least he had married—the only son who did, but to Lee, a Korean woman who barely ever spoke but smiled in admiration of her strange husband, and listened attentively to the wild stories he told about his childhood. Nick was convinced that she was the one who introduced religion into his brother's life and gave him that gift of stability that ended his drift from one place and one job after another.

Of course, the main reason Nick rarely saw him was the distance between them. Seth and Lee had settled finally on a property somewhere in the backwoods Panhandle of Florida, next to the Alabama border, where they raised flowers and sold plants from a small stand adjacent to the highway. Nick had visited a couple of times and thought it was a strange and hard scrabble existence, except for the obvious pleasure the two found in each other, in their husbandry, and in their religion. And he was also quite sure that it was Lee who had talked down her partner's grandiose plans, laughing quietly at his exaggerations and ignoring his blustery outbursts. And it had to be she who had tamed their extravagant tropical environment, laying out neat flower and vegetable gardens, trees burdened with fruit, and rows of laden berry bushes. It was a wonderful place, a refuge, and Nick had been awed by the extravagant beauty she had created.

Of course, his father and mother never made the trip to Florida—it would have been an unpleasant venture for them, and they were perhaps aware of what its consequences would be. His mother would have found a thousand things to rearrange (just helping, of course), while his father would have remained silent and disapproving, sitting in the stiffest chair he could find in their tiny living room. And neither of them would ever understand Lee's gift of peace or the way everything in their lives extended out from their faith.

And Deck? Nick was certain that his brother would have no sympathy for Seth's life. Deck was his father's son—upright, successful, and just as rigid, and he, Nick, was the silent and thoughtful one—the one who always analyzed everything because, well, he felt he was sitting, half amused, on the sidelines watching some spectacle.

"Brotherly love," he mumbled. "Not a lot of that."

On occasion, he had wondered if being tightly wound up in a family where disapproval and intolerance reigned was a key to Deck's success—except that it certainly hadn't worked for him! Just like the motivational speakers hired by the President of his little campus to preach success to its mediocre students, just like a kind of vulgar version of what his parents urged on him.

"*Just believe in yourself,*" these gurus would proclaim, or they might offer THE TEN SIMPLE STEPS TO EARNING THE FORTUNE YOU DESERVE. (The Ten Commandments?)

Achievement, they promised, was uncomplicated if you just believed. It only required a tithe of confidence, they always explained. But because he, Nick, shared so much with his flailing students, he was convinced that they already understood that life held no such easy rewards offered in this optimistic and clichéd advice. Rather, like Deck and his father, it took discipline and denial and, probably, an abbreviated emotional life. How many times had he heard Deck in serious conversation with his father, as they shared their bleak analysis of Seth's failures—how many times had they begun a sentence: "Why can't he...?" And Nick was pretty sure that they repeated the same mantra when they spoke of his own dim prospects as a second-rate musician fiddling away his mediocre talent. And there was even a shadow over Deck, despite his financial success. He was a failure in his father's estimation because he had failed to marry.

It made him wonder about himself: if you were born into a successful family and tried to break away or somehow believed yourself to be different, that you would also have to reject the enthusiasm, drive and discipline that would allow you to repeat their achievements. Or maybe, if you had observed carefully enough when you were a kid, you would decide that you just didn't want to be like them. Perhaps only the unconscious, unthinking, and uncritical child would be able to follow along their same path. Or maybe he just didn't understand any of this at all. All he knew was that in his father's eyes, like his brothers, he had failed. With his pathetic music making! And he'd never have a family either. Perhaps none of them would.

He closed his suitcase and walked out of the bedroom. Moving around his small apartment, he checked to see if the lights were all out and the stove turned off. Glancing into the study, he confirmed that he had put his cello back in its case. He noticed that his music stand held the open pages of a sonata that he had been memorizing, something he might have played for them, except....

His mother had been disappointed when he said he wouldn't bring his cello to the reunion. Their conversation had made him remember when he first became interested in classical music. Neither of his parents played an instrument, or listened to music with much attention, although his mother said for a short time she had sung in the small children's choir at her Methodist Church. And yet he was always curious about the odd symphony he heard on the radio, and he had pestered both parents about taking lessons. That had been the first step, although he was completely unaware at the time, of the way music would estrange him from them.

What he grew to love about the cello, after he settled on the instrument as his choice, was its similarity to the voice and shape of another human being. At first unawares, he developed a kind of unconscious physical affection for its delicate body and beautiful warm wood. After several years of lessons with the music teacher his parents found for him—a woman whose tastes and standards had been so worn down by the sour notes of her pupils that she scarcely paid attention to him—he enrolled in a music school in the City. His father warned him that this was no preparation for a profession, hinting, at the same time, that he probably wasn't good enough. And perhaps Nick realized this all along, but he couldn't simply discard the one thing he had a passion for.

And later he came to realize that the cello was the

only instrument that you hugged to play, and held almost in a sexual embrace between your knees. Its vibrations transmitted by the fingerboard resting on your chest were as resonant as they were erotic: like the frenzied heartbeat of a lover. And when he played, it was always with a deep fondness for the sounds the instrument made. He could not help himself or resist its passion. Whether he was a great, skilled musician or just a passionate amateur, this would always be his joy.

He hesitated at the apartment door, standing next to his suitcase. He realized that all of his thinking and remembering was just a way of postponing his final departure, and if he waited much longer, he would be late to catch the bus. He reached into the closet to grab his coat and then picked up his suitcase. He tried to remember if he had packed his cellphone, and then he remembered that it was still in the bedroom. It would be his lifeline to Mark, his connection to the life he had chosen for himself, and something to grasp onto when he felt himself falling back into the clutches of his family—and becoming again that child he had been once. Just to say hello or read a text message would remind him of his other existence and the person he had chosen to become, and the tentative separation from all of them that he had finally achieved. He ran back to get it before finally closing the apartment door behind him.

A half hour later, he was sitting on an uncomfortable wooden bench in the dingy bus terminal, waiting for the muffled voice of the loud speaker to announce his connection to Champaign. He couldn't remember the number of times he had made this trip, or how many times he had felt a wave of anxiety at the thought of seeing his parents and brothers again. Everyone would be polite (at first); they would ask how he was, even though they had long since given up hope for any real communication. Just words tossed to the wind. And, of course, he would say what he always said: that things were really fine; that his teaching schedule was heavy, but enjoyable. It was just a ritual of meaningless sentences that fended off any serious discussion. And he certainly wouldn't mention the fact that the college had fallen short of its admissions goal for the year, and that staff cuts would be coming. Assuredly, that meant only on his beleaguered side of the campus, where the humanities were shrinking down to a few gut courses taught by several shrewd instructors who kept enrollments lively with gifts of high grades. It was something he couldn't do, and perhaps that marked him for redundancy. It was almost comic that the very things that made his life joyous and rich were disappearing to be replaced by STEM subjects. What an appropriate acronym that was, he thought! When he heard the word, he always imagined a stem without a blossom, a stalk without a single bloom, and something rigid and inanimate and dying.

He was convinced about what was happening at the college, although he couldn't predict the timing. But at the beginning of the semester, the chairman of his section had called him in for a "talk" (which meant that he would be listening to some bureaucratic homily that had translated quite simply into: budget cuts).

He had sat, hands folded, in the bright office with its framed posters of Broadway musicals and signed portraits of opera stars and noted conductors—the collection of a lifetime of being an enthusiastic audience and celebrity buff. (Around the department, the office was referred to as 'the Paparazzi Palace.')

"So glad you stopped in, Nick. I've been wanting to share some information with you."

Fuck the word, "share," he thought.

The chairman paused and then continued, "You've been a valued member of the music department, Nick. Your evaluations have always been acceptable, and the students have appreciated you... apparently." He paused too long on the last word, and Nick thought: *Just like you to begin with a feint of praise—he'd have to share the pun with Mark!—And to phrase your compliments in the past conditional!*

"But," he continued, "I'm sure you realize that the college is facing some financial difficulties. Not that that's anything new. Enrollments have remained steady, but increasingly lopsided, and our side of the campus continues to shrink. And I'll be frank with you, the scientists and engineers are a hungry lot, always wanting new equipment and buildings. I sometimes think that if we could put in for a requisition of technology—microscopes or something new—that we'd earn their respect. But a cello is a cello, and unfortunately, it gets better with age."

Nick said nothing, but just waited to hear the inevitable conclusion.

"So," Ellsworth continued, "I'm going to fight to renew your contract for one more year, at least. That's the best I can promise, but after that, even if I'm successful, and there are certainly no assurances of that, you should plan on finding something else. I'm sorry, but I can't change the way of the world, even if I wished."

Nick had mumbled something about how much he appreciated the efforts of the chairman.

"If I were you," Ellsworth had continued, "I might try my hand at private lessons. Just in the meantime, until something better comes along. You might enjoy it. And it is something. Of course, I'll write you a recommendation. You can count on me."

He wasn't sure how he felt after this interview, probably because he had known the inevitable. In a way that was a relief to know.

He had always realized, of course, that despite his young age, he was already an anomaly and something archaic and left over from an exuberant era that he had only dreamed of but had never experienced—if it had ever truly existed. To be a part of the remarkable world of intelligence and experimental culture he had read about when the young writers, artists, and musicians had made progress from Paris to Vienna, to New York, and to Rome, from salon to gallery to café or to a seaside villa on the Mediterranean. Or after World War II, when New York became the cultural capital of the world, where *experiment* and *modern* were the watchwords. True, he was still relatively young, but what had happened to all those opportunities? However much he yearned for that sort of life, he understood that he was surely living out of such times and beyond the existence he was certain he had been born to inhabit. But, of course, he didn't have the extravagant talent of the smart set. Or the daring to invest his life (and his limited potential) in some foreign adventure. There was a time when he might have risked it. But he didn't. And now, his career had become a diminishing and dissonant chord.

His parents as much as told him so whenever the moment came for their worries to break through the polite euphemisms expressed during his brief visits. It was then that he would remember why he had left at an early age and never really returned—at least never allowing his whole self to be present during these painful encounters with their tactless estimation of him. He was sure that they meant to be helpful, but offering impossible suggestions never helped. And he would not permit them to see the hurt that their disappointment had inflicted on him. Or when they reminded him of his mediocrity. Or the way their careless honesty deflated his dreams. Of course, his mother had tried to be encouraging, despite her misgivings. But his father!

He knew he could not reveal to either of them the threat to his position. Of course, Mark had to know, but that was different. Although *maybe if*—he was almost afraid to finish the thought, not because he should be ashamed to estimate the legacy his father's death might bring him—but maybe it would make it possible and even necessary for him to change, and he would have to face up to his fears, his reluctance, his timidity. *Maybe if* were words that opened the future to frightening possibilities and opportunities

His brother, Seth, had got it right, he thought—Seth, who wrapped himself up inside a kind of imaginary existence, oblivious to the impression he made on others, always seeming self-confident and even domineering, but also pleasantly agreeing to and then ignoring his parents' counsel and criticism. It was strange that among the three brothers, it was Seth who had found a partner who created order in his life—even if he never really recognized it as such—and a wife who introduced him to a religion that made complete sense of the simple beauty of the nature they tended and nourished. Of course he wasn't envious of this nonchalance any more than he resented the financial success about which his brother Deck boasted. And that odd religion? Well, he could never understand that. He had made his own life, and he would have to be content with it even when those unpleasant moments reminded him that he was a second-rate musician, clinging to a crumbling and unsure position, whose ambitions had been diminished with an ever-accumulating series of failed auditions. And yet, he had to admit, there was still Mark. It always came down to that.

The bus trip across the flat, denuded prairie to Champaign only lasted one uncomfortable hour, but he anticipated a long wait for the through train down south. He certainly didn't expect his parents to meet him at the station, so he planned to call an Uber for the drive to the lake. He would probably arrive around dinner time, and he could anticipate that Deck would already be present, but not Seth, of course. You never knew about him—his time and schedule were always his own. But even with his empty chair, they would arrange themselves around the table exactly the way they always did, with his father at the head, Deck on his right, Nick to the left, and his mother closest to the kitchen where she could scurry back and forth to serve. And Seth across from her—a silent and disturbing presence even in his absence.

He thought about all the endless evening meals and the formality of their dinners around the long, cherry wood table. He was sure that his father considered these times to be his opportunity to school his three sons. These lessons had nothing to do with manners or decorum, but with life's probity. It was a ritual that Nick dreaded. He would ask each one of them, in turn, about the day past, about what they had accomplished, what they had learned in school or at playing summer sports. But inevitably, these interrogations would stumble when it came to Seth, who would be trembling with excitement, like a skittish racehorse caught in the anticipation of entering the starting gate, anxious as he was to describe the wonders of his strange and imaginary day. Because Seth lived in a fantasy world, always attuned to the drama that could be created from the most ordinary things, and always, yes always, provoking his father to call him out.

Ritual Interruptus! Nick thought and almost laughed out loud at the phrase. That's what always happened.

"You don't mean what you just said, do you, Seth?" his dad would inevitably declare. "It couldn't have happened that way. Don't exaggerate!"

And Seth would continue on, undaunted, but friendly and happy in his private wonderment until he had outlasted his father, who would just shake his head in exasperation at the wild and fanciful adventures his son recounted. It was, in a way, Nick thought, Seth's effort to belong among the three brothers—to stake his claim. Nick was sure of that. But it always made him seem desperate to impress the indifference of a family that somehow never seemed to fully accept him.

And this evening, even if Seth had not arrived yet, the memory of his oversized presence would sit in his empty chair and irritate them all.

As he traveled in the Amtrak coach burrowing through the cloudy afternoon gloom, he peered out the window, watching the empty fields and farms rush by, interrupted on occasion by the sudden explosion of sound when the train shuddered close to the sides of a bridge or a tower or a crossing. He knew he was concentrating on this moving, noisy panorama because he wanted to avoid thinking about what awaited him at the lake. He was expecting there would be some sort of formal message, an announcement from his father who would not pass up the opportunity to convoke his family. Even if this was to be something grave, as he was certain it would be, his father would choose careful words from his legal lexicon. He would explain everything with precision and without emotion, and that would make it all the more terrible, even if the significance might be difficult to grasp at first. And he would expect them to receive this information in the spirit it was given—as inevitable and as dispassionate as the submission of a brief laid on the podium before a judge. But this reunion wouldn't be a courtroom, nor a legal proceeding—just a family gathering; and different because of what his father would announce. And for once he hoped that his parents might reach out to all of them for solace and comfort, even if he was just as sure this could never happen. Even now.

He anticipated that the two of them, Grace and Richard, would be allied in this endeavor, as they always seemed bound together despite their differences. Neither Nick nor his brothers had ever been able to drive a wedge between their parents, however much they had probed for such an opening. Even Deck, who seemed to be his father's favorite, received his appropriate share of discipline and disapproval from both, although the admonitions of his mother were always soft and gentle. It made Nick wonder about the relationship between his parents. He could never remember an argument between them or unguarded words said in anger. If they ever fought, it had to be with blunted weapons. Although there was that one time, when he passed their bedroom late at night, when he heard his mother sobbing quietly. He had paused for a moment to listen at their door, trying to determine its meaning, but then stumbled back into his room. In the darkness, this sad, muffled noise terrified him as much as the encounter with a ghostly apparition might have done, and he forgot entirely why he was wandering out of his warm bed.

Eventually, he had come to question the permanence of the emotional façade that they had constructed, and the impenetrability of its defenses. And he wondered now about how his father's illness would change things around. Would his father strike out in anger and frustration? Would he be sad? Would he try to be himself when he couldn't be anymore?

By comparison, he and Mark certainly had their disagreements—serious ones on occasion—when they opened their hearts to the corrosion of some serious misunderstanding or hurt. Relationships always had to be adjusted and reconstructed, he thought. They could not be static and remain healthy, if only because the persistence of harmony was limited and certain to expire—the inevitable entropy of love. And yet his parents seemed to have come to some sort of permanent truce, neither one wanting to invade the other's domain—because they were so different and complementary. So old-fashioned, he had to confess, each with a different role to play.

But now he wondered, was everything about to change? Would there be some profound shift? Because his father was seriously ill, would he relinquish the control of his daily life to her? Would she become his monitor, watching over and measuring his advancing deterioration? Would he allow her to touch the diminished core of his strength and determination? Would he allow her to express concern and take control? Would he acknowledge her superior energy and health, and deliver himself to her supervision? And would she even want that after so many years of deference and compromise? It made him wonder what it might be like to deliver yourself into the hands of someone who you had always treated as weaker and subservient. For such a strong man as his father, to give up control and command might be an affront more painful than facing the end. And for her, perhaps, in her, it would awaken an eruption of regrets.

He had been so deep in thought that he did not hear the announcement of his destination, and he only realized it as the train began to slow. Pulling his suitcase from the compartment shelf above his seat, he stood up and made his way toward the end of the car, bumping into the edges of seats along the way as the train swayed to a halt. Once they were stopped, he climbed down the folding metal staircase and stepped onto the gritty concrete of the station. There were several other passengers walking ahead of him, and he watched with mild interest as they spread out through the dingy waiting room of the station, some greeted by relatives or friends, some passing out through the front door and into the cool twilight. He sat down on a bench, pulled out his cellphone and opened the Uber app. Booking his ride, he stood and walked slowly outside to wait. Even these last moments, he thought, were a kind of respite from the revelations he was sure were coming.

On their way to the lake, he asked the driver to detour by the old high school building, the one his father had attended. Even in the gathering dark, the white cement pillars and windowsills stood out from the dingy red brick.

"They're goanna' tear it down soon," the driver said. "You go there or something?"

"No," he replied. "Just someone I know."

"Good memories?"

"Not particularly. Just memories. But I wanted to see it again."

"New building coming up over on West Walnut if you'd like to pass by it too?"

"No thanks," he said. "Just drive on to the lake if you don't mind."

He needed to focus on now and not the past.

CHAPTER 5

The day before they planned to leave for the reunion, Seth and Lee sat at the round Formica table in the kitchen of their bungalow. The bright sun shone through the open window, lighting the limp white curtains that wavered intermittently in the morning breeze. Seth looked at her proudly, taking the measure of her stark black hair, which she had pinned up in the way she knew he liked it. There was something wonderful, he thought, about the way her skin never darkened the way his did, despite her long hours working in the garden. Maybe it was the comical broad-brimmed hat she always wore that deflected the burning Florida sun, but he wanted to believe it was some inner coolness that shielded the freshness of her complexion. To him, she was like some otherworldly forest spirit, whose mysterious touch coaxed commonplace green shoots into exotic blooms. He had come to believe that she was the living proof of God's design. She had given him so much, and he wondered what it was that she had received from him, other than a wildness to be tamed and someone lost whom she had to discover and retrieve.

That was something they would never understand—

not anyone in his family, that is. And he hadn't yet found the words to explain it to them. No matter what he said to them now, they still treated him as they had always done, never quite taking him seriously, even when he wasn't exaggerating, even now, when their obvious and abrupt dismissal of what he said tempted him to be more emphatic. He couldn't help himself when he saw his father's frown and knew that the moment was just seconds away from one of his interruptions: "Now Seth," he would always say, "that just can't be true, can it?" It always sounded like an objection raised in court.

"But, it's true, Sir," he would reply, and then plow on as everyone listened in disbelief. He couldn't help himself.

But the one subject he longed to discuss—his new faith, and how Lee had inspired him—he knew he couldn't even mention that because they had as much as declared that everything he did or believed in was a gross distortion—his religion would be dismissed as a passing enthusiasm. And he refused to humiliate himself because of his beliefs.

How could he describe what she had given him anyway, and how could he explain that everything now seemed to make sense: his life finally defined and accepted? Since he had met her, he could see patterns reflected in everything around him, in all that she touched, from the formal arrangement of their gardens—the neat beds of luxuriant flowers and the dark green, almost black leaves of broccoli, cabbages, and lettuce—to his salvaged soul. That was the joyous vision that redemption had brought him, and the faith that possessed and reclaimed him.

At first, he could scarcely contain the story of his rebirth, even though he knew it would be a mistake to proclaim it. He had sent pamphlets and long letters to his brothers, describing the new peace and purpose in life that he had discovered. At the beginning, they had only ignored him, but he persisted because he believed that each of them, in his own peculiar way, was as much a lost soul as he had once been. And so he kept on, determined to salvage even one of them and rescue someone close to him from the unhappiness he was sure they suffered, that they might rejoice with him. But then, what a disappointment it had been that Nick, first, and then Deck, had finally written polite, firm letters (as if they had agreed together on this strategy) saying how pleased they were that he had found a stillness after so much turmoil and chaos in his life, and so many disappointments and failures, but they would tend to their own souls and didn't require his advice. Nick had even added a postscript to one of his letters, citing a book that purported to reveal the folly and corruption of his faith. His first reaction had been anger, but that eventually softened into disappointment. Nick of all people! He wouldn't say anything to his face, but he told Lee that of his two brothers—wayward Nick was the one who needed saving the most.

"Do you know why your parents insisted that you come?" Lee asked as she stood up to clear away the dishes. "What about the church? I mean, can you leave right now, just when you've earned a position of leader? Won't the elders want you to remain? I know it's something you wanted for a long time, and now, just when you're about to begin, you have to leave. It's such bad timing."

"But it's my family, Lee."

"But the way they treat you? And you're really needed here. It's such a bad moment to abandon the people who depend on you."

"There isn't ever a good time, is there? I don't care what happens when we're all together again. I mean that I do care. I care absolutely. But this is an obligation I can't just avoid, even if I wanted to. It's family."

"Well, I'm sure you know best."

"So Lee, you have to promise me: you won't mention anything to anyone—my parents. I'll tell them if and when I'm ready. And maybe it'll be just one more thing piled on everything else to them, and they'll say: 'He's so strange! Why is he throwing his life away? Religion? And now he's about to be some kind of minister? How did that happen?' But this trip has to be about them, not me."

"You know best, Seth."

"And I'm pretty sure that Dad is sick, real sick. Not that they said anything specific. They never really say the words outright. But I could tell. Mom sounded sad and exhausted on the phone, and she said it was for him—she wanted all of us brothers to see him, without, of course saying: *for the last time*. So, of course I told her we'd both come."

"Did she say anything about that?"

"What?"

"About me...I mean when you said I'd be there too."

"No. Of course not. I'd never go without you."

"But you know they don't like me very much. They think—I don't know—they think I've made you weird or something."

"Come on Lee! You rescued me."

"I don't know, Seth. They just don't seem to like me very much."

"I don't think they'd show their feelings no matter what they felt. Everyone in my family is always hiding who they really are. I mean, Nick! For God's sake! And Deck. Who knows anything about him, really? Just a bunch of strangers stranded in a family.

"When I think about it," he continued, "... all those times when I was growing up. Mom and Dad were always trying to change all of us, but me, especially. Made me think that both of them must have had a really unhappy childhood. I never could do anything right—at least in their eyes. And Dad, well, I don't think he ever looked at me without disappointment smeared like guilty jam all over his face. And what made it worse was that I knew he was trying. He gave me a hundred chances to grow up to be just like him. All those aptitude tests I had to take and the counselors and special classes! You know he wanted me to be smart in school, go on to college, become a lawyer, or whatever. But as for me, well, I guess I failed him all the time because I never had any interest in those things. He never said it outright, and I don't know what I would have done if he had, but he knew, and I knew that he believed it was because I was adopted, and he couldn't face the fact that I'd always be someone different. He tried—they both tried, Mom too—to make me just like them, but I couldn't be. And, you know, Lee, I really didn't want to be. Even possible that all their efforts made me want to be a failure in their eyes."

He stopped for a minute to sip the dregs of his coffee and then stood up to hand her the cup.

"How can you ever succeed in being someone you aren't destined to be? And I really believe that God has special plans for everyone," he said, putting his arms around her. "And now that I'm finally happy and the person I was always supposed to be, well, they've just given up on me and don't want to know me. Thank God I've got you!"

"Well, I do understand, Seth," she said, turning off the faucet and putting the last plate into the dish drainer. "But then you married a foreigner to make it all worse!!"

"That doesn't matter. Not at all."

"Well, it's a feeling I get sometimes. I'm sure they have all sorts of questions they want to ask me, but they're afraid that they won't understand or like what I'm answering. What was it like growing up in Korea? What my parents was like? And my first husband? Are you really comfortable living in a strange country? Why'd you get divorced? Don't you ever want to go back? And what they really want to know: did you get married to that G.I. back then just so you could come to the US?"

"I'm sure they're too uptight or polite to ask anything like that, so I guess they'll just have to imagine all the answers for themselves."

"And they probably don't like what they're thinking, I'm sure of that."

"Look, Honey. It's just them. It has nothing to do with you."

"It's got everything to do with me," she said.

"Well, you don't have to go, then, if you don't want to."

"Of course I want to. I have to. You need me to be there if you're going."

"How come you're so certain of that?"

"I just am," she said. "You know you! Now make sure you got everything packed up in the camper. I'm ready in just a minute."

"You're right, of course. I wouldn't want to go without you, Lee."

"I know that. Now *skedaddle*."

He reached over and put his hand on her face.

"I love it when you try to talk slang! Like a Korean cowboy," he said. "From watching American westerns when you were a kid?"

"I always loved American movies. Now let go!" she replied, twisting away. "You're just trying to make us late."

"You're right; I just want a few more minutes. I'd much rather be alone with you."

"Watch out, Mister hombre, Señor Seth. I just might.... But really, I'll take one last look around and meet you out in the camper. Don't make us late!" she exclaimed.

He just laughed and walked out of the kitchen to carry the suitcases into the camper.

An hour later, they had finally emerged out from the last of the county roads, covered by a dense canopy of live oaks and dangling, silver-grey Spanish moss, bordered by stunted palmettoes. They reached the first of several connecting Interstate highways, heading north and slightly to the west toward the southern tip of Illinois. It would be ten hours straight through, and they had already argued about whether to stop midway. Seth declared that he could drive the whole way—he told her that he had once made it cross country without sleeping, but Lee insisted that they find a Walmart and spend the night in their parking lot. Of course, he knew she was right, but he thought it would make a grand story to tell the family if they made it in one shot. Deck and Nick would never dare an adventure like that.

Seth always remembered whenever they traveled north, back to the time when they were newly married and living in the backwoods behind St. Louis in his trailer.

He'd come a long way since then: no—he was wrong; they had made this journey together. How could he ever forget that?

He had met Lee in a little roadside restaurant where she was working as a waitress. He didn't pay much attention to her at first, but eventually found himself taking a slight detour every so often on his way out to construction jobs just to be around her. In the beginning, he was curious more than anything, to find this young woman from Korea handing out plates of St. Louis-style ribs and cheeseburgers and crinkle-cut fries. Of course, he realized it wasn't strange at all—not for the US anyway. His brief stint in the army had taught him that. From the first day even, when all the recruits stood naked waiting for their physical and he looked around, he had thought that there was every shape and color and type all jumbled up together, like assorted jelly beans in a drugstore jar. It almost made him laugh even now to think about it.

He realized that he had been the shy one around Lee. At first, anyway. Because, when he finally got up enough nerve to ask her out, she had said yes as if she had been expecting it. In the beginning, they were clumsy together, nevertheless. He hadn't known what to say to her, and he held back about asking her how she had come to this small, dead-end, hard-shoulder café. But eventually, when they were living together, she recounted a story that made him really angry and, he guessed, looking back on it, wanting to make it up to her somehow.

He had to coax her to begin, but he really wanted to know—so that he could understand her. So he planned it for a time when they sat together, in the front seat of his camper, in the gathering dark, where he had felt that it was much easier for her to talk and when he wouldn't be able to see her face clearly. But once she began, she told him a long story. And from the way she talked on and on, her voice full of emotion, hesitating and doubling back like a lost hiker looking to regain the trail, he had the feeling that she had never told anyone about her life before.

At first she was reluctant to say much about her childhood in Korea or her family, but it was pretty clear they didn't have much. And she told how she left home, traveling up to the Osan American Air Force Base, not far from Seoul, where she had grown up. Pushed out of the house when she was old enough, she explained, because there wasn't enough for all of them, she found a job there in the American Canteen. She didn't like it at first; hated it, in fact. The G.I.'s scared her, she said, because they were so big and loud and much too friendly. She couldn't understand their lack of formality, their pushiness, and the way they called each other strange names that she later learned had to do with some country or other that their family came from or something about sex. Always something about sex. It was a strangeness that made no sense to her, especially because she couldn't see any of the differences that seemed so important to them. They just all looked alike to her, and behaved the same.

But she did understand from the way several of them talked to her and stared at her, what they wanted, so she was careful to keep to herself distant, with her eyes down, and pretending not to hear the crude, threatening words that she was quickly learning to understand. She told Seth that she finally realized what she had to do to protect herself, and that meant to accept one of the men as a sponsor and a lover. She chose a lonely, sad-looking boy who seemed to stand apart from the others. She found it easy to talk to him and be with him.

Nothing changed at first, and the leers and rough jokes at the Canteen continued. But gradually, the other Americans seemed to recognize that Daniel (that was his name) had taken possession of her. At least she thought of it that way, but secretly, she understood that she had clutched him tightly to her and to the plan that she scarcely wanted to confess to herself.

"I am ashamed of myself," she explained to Seth. "I made him love me because I wanted, more than anything, to come to America. I know that was a strange thing. I didn't like Americans, and I thought they were cruel and loud and vulgar. But there was nothing left for me in Korea. My parents were too poor to arrange a marriage, and no money for the *Yedan* and all the gift giving you have to do. And I had no possibility for education, either. Who would pay for me? So what could I do but leave? I wanted to become a new person in a new place. That was my plan. And I thought it would be easy, because I had learned so much English from talking to all the soldiers.

"I don't know who was the first one to say something about marriage; maybe, I think, he did. But I have no memory. So, we began to talk about future living together. In America. I almost thought that I could love him, even though he always seemed to be just an innocent, lost boy.

"I know this was a wrong thing to do, but maybe he was wrong too. And he insisted to marry in Korea. At first I didn't understand why. And it is always difficult there with foreigners. There were many permissions to get. But finally we did. My parents would not come to the wedding on the base, and my father called me a terrible name. But

I didn't care. I was going to be free."

When she recounted this, Lee stopped and looked at Seth. She wondered if it would hurt him that she had been with someone else. That she was so strong wanting to come to America. But he reached over and gripped her hand tightly... still.

"It was only later," she said, "when we came to America, that I understood why Daniel wanted to marry in Korea. Because his parents too, were angry that he would marry someone who looked like me. A foreigner. He was always very afraid of them, and he worried they would force him to leave me. And when I finally met them, it was a terrible time. So many silences and looks that hurt me. We sat in their dark living room. I even thought that they feared turning on the lights would mean they had accepted me. Or let me see how they lived. And just like that, all possible happiness stayed hidden in the shadows of their disapproval. They said almost nothing to me; they hardly looked at me; but when they spoke to Daniel, they were so cruel. But I could see that their knives came out for me. And he tried to be brave at first, but, you see, he was too weak. I realized that, and I wanted so much to be here—to stay forever. But he wouldn't stand up against them. Even when we moved near St. Louis, away from them and their looks that stabbed. I knew he was still feeling their anger and meanness burning inside him. They would never leave him alone.

"For a while, he tried to be happy, but he became a stranger, almost like a person I didn't know, and we were just two people living in a tiny house. I was so lonely. I had no one to help me or talk to. Still, I tried. But his parents' picture of me had sneaked inside him, and made him blind.

"Yes, sometimes he just looked through me like I was some ghost. We both knew that it had been a terrible mistake, but we stayed together for too long a time, because not knowing what to do. I think Daniel feared to leave, to admit that his parents were right. He was afraid to confess he had made a terrible mistake. And I knew nothing about your American laws. Finally, he decided on a divorce and took me to a lawyer's office. I just signed the papers without reading them. I had no idea what they said except that they meant we were no longer married. And he went away. And I never saw him again."

Seth stopped her, reached down and put his other hand on top of hers. He knew he shouldn't interrupt, but something in the sadness of what she was saying made him interrupt her.

"So you decided to stay near St. Louis?" he asked.

"Well," she said, "I had to move out of the house we lived in, you understand, where I tried to make us a life, and I found a room and my job. There are some other Koreans in St. Louis, all in one small place in the city. I knew that because once Daniel took me to a restaurant there—when he was trying to make me happy. But I didn't want to be around them. And I decided I would be able to learn the American language even better if I was alone, and then I might even find American friends. But that wasn't what happened. But I learned lots of English from watching TV, and I found lots of new words from watching ads, and western movies, and quiz shows, but I never did make a lot of friends. I mean real friends. That was much harder. That was my story until I met you."

Mulling over what she told him when he asked her to marry, several months after they had met, Seth understood why Lee was terrified to meet his parents and face, once again, the hostile looks and misunderstandings that she was convinced any American family would let slip as soon as they saw her. She told him how frightened she was. But after he took her across the river to the town where his parents had retired, she was surprised that his mother and father greeted her with unexpected joy, almost with relief. Eventually, she came to realize that they were most concerned about Seth—that they worried about him and, in fact, his mother said to her once when they were alone that she always feared what would happen to him. He had been such a wandering boy and needed stability. She had hopes for him now.

Seth had moved her sparse belongings into his trailer on a small rented property after their wedding out in the countryside around St. Louis. They had married before a judge because he hated ceremony, and she was happy enough not to pretend to be an American bride like she had seen on television, with a long white dress, blonde hair, white skin and white flowers.

But Lee found that she was alone again with only her garden and her television set, because Seth left for days at a time on construction jobs, and she remained by herself on a half acre of land surrounded by woods. Nonetheless, she was determined to make every sunny patch bloom, and gradually she willed this abandoned, packed-down spread of clay and patchy scrub into a garden with tidy rows of vegetables, trellises drooping with clusters of grapes and sweet-smelling wisteria, round beds of flowers, and the beginnings of a small orchard. This was not an easy task because she had to battle the crows that dug up her seeds, groundhogs and rabbits who nibbled away tender shoots as soon as they emerged, and deer that trampled everything as they ate away the emerging leaves of young trees.

Finally, Seth bought her a rangy Labrador puppy to be her gardener's assistant, and his mock ferocity and clumsy chases restored her dominion over this small, isolated green paradise.

But still, she was by herself much of the time. Still alone in a country that seemed unwelcoming and empty. There were few close-by neighbors, and although she tried to be friendly, anyone she casually encountered was merely polite and usually busy. That is, until one day a visitor appeared who changed both of their lives.

She had been working outside in the noonday sun, her face hidden by her large, floppy hat, with her dog (Si-Woo) lying beside her, belly up, soaking up the heat. Suddenly, he stood up and barked faintly, and Lee looked toward the dusty road that led onto their property. She could see an elderly woman emerging along the path and treading carefully, almost as if she was leaning on a cane.

Lee waved to her, grabbed the collar of Si-Woo, and commanded him to stay, as she hurried to greet her visitor.

As she approached, she could see that the woman was sweating from the exertion of her long walk, and that she was carrying a small black bag that looked like a shoulder briefcase. She stopped, took out a large white cloth and wiped her face. And then she smiled:

"Wasn't sure there'd be folks at the end of this road," she said. "But I got curious and strolled on out. Never know what you're about to find if you're curious. And what a place you got here. My oh my! Why it's like God's Garden of Eden. Never thought I'd see such a sight back in these here dark Missouri backwoods!"

She stopped to catch her breath, and then continued: "And strange to find someone like you here if you don't mind me commenting. Why, I'd almost think I'd wandered into some foreign country. But here I am. And I'm bringing you good tidings from Jesus."

Lee was surprised and pleased to greet this strange woman, and invited her to sit on the little brick patio that Seth had laid out behind the trailer while she made a pot of tea. There they remained for several hours until dark began to hover over their conversation, and then the woman stood up abruptly and opened her satchel.

"I've got the printed Word of God here for you, young lady, and I'll leave a tract or two behind for you to study up on if you don't mind," she said. "And if it will be all right with you, I'll come back from time to time, just to see how you're getting on, and so we can talk some more about the Pathway."

"The pathway?" asked Lee.

"Why yes, my dear, the one that goes right on up to Heaven. The straight and narrow!"

At first Lee was reluctant to tell Seth very much about her new and frequent visitor. But she did nothing to hide the pamphlets that Mrs. Montrose (her name) dropped in her hand for her to consider, and she even encouraged him to read one or two of them.

"Pretty much hogwash," he said at first. "Next thing you know they'll be begging us for money. Build themselves some big new church they just got to have or buy the minister a shiny black Cadillac because he can't drive his old Ford one mile further."

"She never did ask for a single Won, Seth, and never even mentioned anyone else. I like her."

"Well, watch out anyhow," he said. "I remember back when I was a kid that my mom dragged my dad and all of us to church for at least two sermons a year: Christmas Eve for show, since the whole town would be eyeing who was in attendance, and Donor's Sunday to soften him up for a contribution. That pretty much summed up the extent of my family's faith."

"But she's different, Seth," she said. "Don't be so quick on the draw to be judging my friend and her religion. She's a very fine woman, and I'm sure there's not a dishonest bone in her."

Lee didn't encourage Seth during the next few months—at least not openly. But often when he returned home, sweaty and tired from a construction job, there would be new pamphlets carefully planted around the small trailer, and hard to miss. And he got the habit of asking her for the latest ones, just out of curiosity, he said. And they took to discussing them because Seth was beginning to see the Design that she was helping him to notice. After several months, they ventured to the nearby Kingdom Hall, and he couldn't help but be taken by the friendly welcome they received. After that first venture, Seth sat Lee down in the small corner of their trailer, turned off the TV that was usually humming, and took her hand in his:

"You know, Lee, I've been worrying about you being all by yourself back here in the woods. Not afraid for your safety, 'cause you got your dog and all, but fearful that you'd be lonely and lonely'd make you sad and homesick, and I couldn't stand that. But I have to tell you now that it's me that's been lonely all along. I guess I was all by myself and apart as a kid, not really belonging in my family, and then later, well, I'd already learned to be separated from folks."

She interrupted: "But Seth, you're the friendliest man I've ever met."

"Just seems that way, Honey, because I like to tell stories, but down inside, well, there's a different feeling. I'm all tied up in knots there. At least I realize that now. But for the first time, aside from with you, of course, I feel like I might belong somewhere. And I'm talking about those religious folks.... It just makes you think different to be among them—more like your true self."

As they drove into the gathering dusk, finally reaching southern Tennessee, Lee located a Walmart on her cellphone where they could park the camper overnight. It was twilight when they pulled in. This wasn't the first time they found themselves in such a place as part of a small encampment of trailers and trucks preparing to bed down for the night. Seth loved these transient gatherings of highway nomads—strangers come together to share a temporary citizenship, but knowing they'd never, ever meet again. Somehow that made everyone friendly, he thought, like they were all chosen to come together as part of some great adventure. As usual, while Lee heated up their dinner on the small propane stove in the camper, Seth strode out to chat with some of the folks who were gathering around outdoor grills, or just sitting in lawn chairs staring up at the sky and conversing in low tones.

A couple, maybe, were drinking a soft drink or two and just enjoying the fading warmth, or maybe he'd see a lonely trucker sitting in the cabin with the door open, can of beer in his hand, and his feet dangling out. As he always did, he carried a small clutch of tracts. He had his favorites, especially the one about God's Design—the one with the picture of a dinosaur and a caveman on the cover and the proof that Evolution was just an atheist's folly. It wasn't that he was trying to convert anyone to anything in this accidental city of strangers. His only real purpose was to share the joy that his new faith had brought him. But when someone tried to engage him, positive or negative, it didn't matter which. He'd be happy enough to stop and chat for a while. He vowed never to argue the point, because he'd learned that most people got to be stubborn when you contradicted them, usually trying to think of ways to catch you up or put you down. No, there was not much purpose in that. It was just his own happiness he wanted to share. It seemed like he couldn't restrain himself.

When he finally returned to the camper, the inside would be warm from the stove, and he could almost feel the heavy smell of dinner already. Lee never asked him about his talks, but she knew he'd tell her the parts he wanted to.

It was late when they sat down at the small pull-out counter and began to eat.

"Ran into this neat old guy and his wife sitting over behind that big semi," he said suddenly. "Turned out that he was one of us. Coming down from Kentucky on their way down to Florida. Imagine that! All of us heading in opposite directions but, you know, really traveling to the same place. Makes you wonder."

Lee was silent and just nodded.

"Something the matter, honey?" he asked.

"Just this trip," she began. "Your whole family. Contemplating them."

"Nothing for you to fret about."

"It's not me; I don't care much about that," she said.

"You. It's you that's got me mostly worried."

"Tell you what," he said, wiping his mouth with a paper napkin. "Just think of it as a visit like to this parking lot, here."

"Seth," she said. "Sometimes you don't make no sense at all. You're always pulling such strange ideas outa' your holster!"

"Whoa! Slow down, cowgirl," he said, laughing. "I just mean, you should just think of it as if you really didn't know anything about my family—a chance meeting with some old folks, like here in the Walmart parking lot. Strangers come together by accident. Try to think of them as if you hadn't ever met before. I sometimes do. And it helps—it helps me to forget the past. And it gives me hope."

When they finished eating and Lee had washed the plates and utensils, they strolled out into the cool evening. The glare of the store security lights bleached the sky grey, and only a few stars and a sliver of moon were visible. Most of the other temporary residents had retreated inside their trailers or the cabs of trucks for the night. The scattered vehicles cast long shadows on the asphalt. The only noise was the distant whoosh of traffic from the nearby Interstate. Seth took Lee's hand almost without realizing it and pulled her to a halt.

"You know, this has got to be my favorite time of day—early night, that is, when things are settling down. I love looking up at the stars and thinking Who made them and all. And how beautiful it all is."

"But Seth, you can scarcely see any stars tonight; it's so cloudy."

"I know that, Honey. But the thing is, I always know

they're sitting up there; like God himself."

The next morning they resumed their drive toward the southern tip of Illinois. As they traveled on, something Lee said reminded Seth of an unpleasant family dinner. It was an uncomfortable memory that often returned to him when he least expected or wanted it—like a bad feeling he couldn't dismiss. It was nothing more than a stupid child's memory, and he tried not to allow it to bother him, but that only made it more intense. Maybe it was the name Indian Hills, Kentucky, that made him remember when she noticed it come up on the GPS and asked him if there were actually Indians living there.

He had been about eleven or twelve, not that it mattered exactly, although he'd surely recall exactly if he thought hard about it. But all of them were sitting at the dining room table, his father at the end, Deck and Nick to the right and left of him, and he and his mother across from each other at the other end. Like every other night, his father quizzed each of them about their day, around the table, one after the other, clockwise. Deck and Nick were always shy and answered as little as possible, but that night Seth had been excited. That wasn't uncommon. In fact, during almost every dinner, he loved to talk, except that for the same, unavoidable reason, it always ended the same way, with his father glaring at him and correcting what he said. Questioning and doubting him. But that night especially, Seth wanted to tell about the Indian relics he thought he'd found in the creek just out of town where he had ridden his bicycle.

He couldn't help himself, even though he knew in advance that it would bring trouble, but he announced that he had found several arrow heads.

"Must have been a big battle there," he said. "I'm sure if I go back I'll find some more relics—maybe even a piece of pottery."

His father just looked at him for a minute and then said: "Are you sure, Seth? You're not exaggerating?"

"No, sir. I'm pretty certain of what I found."

"But I don't believe there are any Indian remains near here. Not that I know of. Are you certain? Maybe you can show us?"

"Well, I left them there. Didn't know what to do with them. Wasn't sure I ought to take them."

"Seth!" his father said, slamming his hand on the table. "You're always talking, just crazy talk. You didn't find anything, did you?"

"I'm sure I did," he said. "At least there were some stones that looked like they were pointed."

"You're excused from the table. You can go to your room. Now!"

Seth had reluctantly left his half-finished dinner and gone to his room, where he sat on the bed wondering about himself. Why had he done it? So many dinners ended abruptly, just like that. Why was he always saying things that upset his father? Maybe they *were* just stones and not arrow heads like he said. But he couldn't help himself. His brothers seemed so comfortable, and both parents beamed at them with pride for no reason at all—even when they were being critical. And he wanted his parents to be proud of what he did, too. But they always seemed disappointed. You could see it on their faces. And they were so quick to disapprove.

Maybe, in their own way, they tried and he certainly tried, but somehow they were caught up in some sticky web of disappointment. No—it wasn't that, exactly. They let him know, in ways that were plain enough to see, that he was a failure, and that everything he tried to do fell short of what they wanted and expected of him. He could scarcely count the ways: his trouble in high school, then a dropout after his first, unsuccessful semester in college (and his father had to pull strings to get him into the state school), two years in the army with no promotion, his jobs—so many different ones that even he had lost track. He wanted to think that their hopes for him had been a kind of love. He still did, sometimes, but he feared that their deliberate love had soured into permanent exasperated looks and regrets. It had sometimes made him hate himself—at least until he found Lee and the gift of faith she had led him to.

And he wondered now, driving toward this reunion, if they would ever let him be himself, to really see him as he had become now. If he dared to tell them.... How wonderful it would be if they understood and could participate in his joy. Or was it true that the more he became who he was always intended to become, the less they would accept his life's mission?

"You're awfully silent," Lee said, reaching over to rub his neck gently. "Are you tired of driving?"

"No. Not at all. Just thinking."

"I am too," she said. "And worrying. Will it be awful?"

"No. Nothing out of the ordinary. It'll just be them."

"Oh," she said, looking out the window at the unrevealing land.

CHAPTER 6

The slant of morning light was so bright in the kitchen that Grace, sitting at the table, had to shade her eyes from the glare. But she made no effort to pull the window shades closed. This early in the day, when the October sun was hovering low to the horizon, the brightness would only be momentary. Short days meant quick days, when the sun shot with reckless speed across the low arc of sky. And she loved to feel the momentary heat on her hands—old hands that never seemed warm anymore; and that felt like someone else's fingers when she touched something.

Richard would probably sleep a while longer, despite the coming excitement of the day. But when he woke, she would have to help him up—help him to dress and then be his crutch into the kitchen.

She looked around. The coffee pot was simmering on the stove. His cereal box was set next to his place. There was a bowl of oranges at the center of the table, and just next to it, in front of where he would sit, was the slim plastic case that held his pills, a separate section for each day of the week, and filled with what looked like multi-colored candies: red, blue, green, and orange: one shade for each debility. She wondered, for a moment, if the drug companies had agreed to divide up the spectrum, each medicine with a proprietary hue, completing a sad rainbow of disease.

He would call to her in a minute, but she treasured these quiet moments by herself. Perhaps she wouldn't hear him at first. She needed to be alone, and this was the only opportunity. It seemed that ever since his illness worsened, she had no time left to be on her own. Theirs had become a strange kind of companionship where he was entirely dependent on her. And she knew that for him, this was the worst and most frustrating part of his illness—not to be dominant and strong and independent. But she felt that this upending in their relationship was just an added burden for her.

Especially today, he would make every effort to be firm and in control, whatever the cost, because this would be his final attempt to impose on all their futures. He was going to use his death as a bond to secure them to his departing wishes. She had argued against this too many times already. Once even daring to accuse him of seeking some strange afterlife by enforcing his last wishes. But as his physical strength diminished, he seemed more and more adamant about using his absence as an unbreakable promise that would outlast his final breath. It wasn't that he desired immortality. He denied that. He was certainly not a religious man. They had both long relinquished any belief in eternity. It was just a habit that he couldn't abandon, and the result was this odd, unwelcome legacy to her and his sons.

She heard him call her name, softly at first—still weak from sleep. For a moment, she ignored him. But finally, she stood up and walked slowly into the hall leading to their bedroom. She wanted to arrive by his side before the sound of his voice became desperate.

When they were finally sitting in the kitchen, and some of the breakfast dishes were in the sink, Richard looked more energetic and there was color on his face, if in blotches.

"I'm sure Deck will be here any time now. If I know him, he left early and he'll drive like hell."

"I worry about that," she said.

"Among other things, am I right? Are you going to ask him if this girl—I suppose he'll bring someone—if she's the one... finally?"

"If I can get him alone. I don't know if today's the right time to say anything. It's your day, not mine."

She thought for a moment that she had emphasized the last two words too abruptly. She didn't intend to be harsh, but deep inside her, she knew she was furious at him. He had become so weak and yet even more determined at the same time. It was an unnatural mix of emotions, and she was afraid of what he might say or do. And who knew how his sons would react? She feared the worst.

She was reminded that lately she had been thinking about the word *abuse*, and returning often to consider what it meant, and whether it had somehow taken residence inconspicuously in their relationship. Suddenly the word seemed to be everywhere, or at least she noticed it now: in the newspaper, on television, in the magazines she read: so much so that it almost seemed to describe the only way people related to each other anymore. Maybe she shouldn't take seriously the articles she read about couples who clawed at each other's egos. Or parents or other adults who abused children. But the discussion seemed to be everywhere. And it had made her rethink her relationship with Richard. And his with their sons. Of course, he had never struck them—and certainly neither had she. But she wondered if the absence of kindness was some sort of insidious cruelty—emotional abuse would be the word for it—and if it had afflicted them all, making them timid about trusting their feelings, withdrawn, and self-doubting. He had always been so determined and right—righteous—and perhaps it was the unceasing working of his integrity and pride that had worn down their spontaneity.

She asked herself, in these moments of contemplation, if she still loved him, and if she ever had, or if what existed between them had become some kind of joint tenancy, just dwelling in a partnership of parallel duties. She would probably never know for sure unless, in the years that lay before her, without him, she might come to free herself from the tenacity of memory long enough to be honest. If he would let her... if the terms of his will would not imprison her and all of them within his continuing authority. For a moment, she hoped that being free...

"You seem lost in thought," he said, pushing away his half-empty bowl. "You need to help me. I've got to accomplish this last thing."

"I know it's going to be difficult with everyone here," she said. "Especially Seth. You mustn't let him tire you out."

"I can't promise anything if he starts to preach that crazy gospel of his. And that wife of his! So strange and almost invisible. She never says anything; just looks at him with those admiring eyes."

"Well, I hope you won't let him get to you."

"Get at me, you mean?"

"Well, yes, I suppose. But I think he means well."

"And just look at what a life of good intentions has brought him—a jungle plot, living in a trailer, selling whatever it is the two of them can eke out of the ground from a roadside stand. How's that for an inconsequential life? When we gave him every advantage and look what he did with it. Smashed it all! Not that Deck and Nick are perfect, either. Where are they, by the way? Shouldn't they be here by now?"

She said nothing, hoping that her silence, and the way she often pretended to be absent, to avoid answering him, would tamp down his anger. She refused to be his echo this morning.

He was quiet for a minute, looking blankly at her, and then struggled to stand up.

"I need your help, Grace. I want to be in the living room when they come."

"All right," she said.

She walked slowly with him, one shuffling step after another, allowing him to lean on her shoulder as she maneuvered him to the sofa. She said nothing, but she could tell, from the weight he shifted onto her, that he was weaker today, as if the strain of the upcoming encounter with his sons had already exhausted his energy.

"At least it's a partly sunny day... warm," he said. "At least there's that."

"Yes," she said, sitting on the chair facing him.

"And tomorrow, if the weather holds, we'll take the boat out and do some fishing."

"Must you, Richard? Are you up to it? Don't you think...?"

He said nothing, and she understood that this excursion would be an excuse to be alone with his sons, out of earshot of the women who would remain in the house. He wanted to tell them, on his own and in his particular way, what he had planned and why. And he wanted them to know what was in store for him. She wondered if doing something energetic like fishing, or pretending to, was his way of allowing them to hide their reaction, to distract them from the grief about the progress of his disease as he explained it to them. Or surely the anger and surprise when he told them his plans. He had decided that it was an act of kindness to allow all of them to suppress their feelings in the repressive seclusion of maleness.

"What time is it?" he asked.

"It's early still. Only about ten," she said, looking out over the lake through the large picture window, as if her attention was fixed on some distant point. "I don't think anyone will arrive before noon. So why don't you take a nap? I can get you a blanket if you're cold."

She started toward him, but he waved her away.

"Why don't you look out back and see if anyone's here yet."

"All right," she said, turning and walking out of the room.

She entered the kitchen, and then opened the door that faced into the rear of their property and the driveway. There was nothing remarkable to see, only the sun gleaming on the cement and a portion of the twisted paved road under the trees that led up to it. She inhaled the cool air and then closed the door with an extra effort. And then she almost laughed out loud at herself, realizing that she had pulled the door shut loudly enough so that he would hear it and know that she had done as he asked. Was she that fearful of his temper? Even now? Or did she intend it as a kindness and reassurance? It was strange how his illness had changed everything around, and uncovered so many thoughts that might have remained buried forever. Or perhaps, she mused, these might be new ideas and a new understanding of the connection between them that she had always simply taken for granted and was now about to be broken.

She returned to the living room, walking cautiously because she thought he might be dozing. Stopping under the archway that led into the room, she could see that he was slouched over on the sofa, his eyes half shut, the way a predatory animal slept, half alert to any passing opportunity. How sad it was, then, she thought, that in these final days, he had become so weak and dependent on her.

After his stroke and the months of debilitating struggle to regain something of his old energy and mobility, he had suffered a serious cardiac arrest, and the specialist from St. Louis had warned them both that his weakened heart would probably last only a few more months. Unsurprising death could come at any moment. What a strange thing it was, she thought, to contemplate that just one part of you was dying inside you—that you had a single fatal flaw that would shut down everything else that was still functioning perfectly.

He sighed briefly and then sat up abruptly. "Anyone here yet?" he said, catching sight of her. "Did you even look?"

"Yes, of course, I just came from the back door. No one has arrived yet."

"You'd think someone would be here by now. After all, they promised."

"Don't worry, Richard. They'll be here shortly. Can I get you anything?"

"No... and please stop looking at me that way."

"What way is that Richard?"

"Like I'm to be pitied."

"Sorry, I didn't mean..."

"And maybe I'll take that blanket now. I'm feeling chilly all of a sudden."

Without a word, she turned and headed toward the large linen closet in the hallway in front of their bedroom. But she stopped, reminding herself to look into the other two bedrooms again to confirm that everything had been laid out for Nick and Deck and whoever might be tagging along with him. She had put out towels already, and checked the clean sheets twice or three times already this morning, but she glanced into both bedrooms once more, just to be sure. When she had verified that everything was ready, she picked out a small quilt from a neat pile of blankets in the closet and returned to the living room. Richard had dozed off again, so she gently tucked the quilt around his shoulders and propped a pillow under his right arm in the direction he was leaning.

Just a moment later, she heard the approach of a car and then a door slamming shut and then another behind the house. She walked quickly into the kitchen and then outside. Deck and a woman she didn't recognize were just unloading the trunk of his car, pulling out suitcases and resting them on the driveway.

She rushed over to embrace him, maybe more enthusiastically than he expected, because he stepped back.

"This is Susan," he said, pushing his companion forward, as if she was a shy child. "My mother."

"Oh, please call me Grace," she said.

"And I'm Susan Barone." She paused. "I'm very happy to meet you. Deck has told me so much about the family."

"I hope not too much," Grace said, trying to force a smile. "But do come in now. You must be tired after such a long drive. I'll fix you something to eat if you want. But at least I can get you an iced tea. Or maybe a coffee. You must have gotten up very early."

"Don't go to a lot of trouble, please, Mom," Deck said, picking up the two suitcases. "We'll just put these inside. And maybe we'll have a coffee later."

He started toward the door and then stopped, as if he remembered something: "So how's he doing?"

"Not very well, I'm afraid. But he'll want to tell you himself."

Susan looked at Deck for a moment, and started to say something, but he just turned away and walked up the two steps to the door, shouldering it open, and entered the kitchen, carrying the two suitcases. She followed him inside.

"Your mother seems pleasant," she said, once they were alone in the bedroom.

"She's nice enough," Deck said, hoisting his charges onto the bed.

"Is this your old room?" she asked.

"Yes and no. I didn't grow up here, of course. But I guess it's mine since I sleep here whenever I visit."

"And the lake was really lovely—what I could see of it when we passed alongside it. You must really love it here."

He just looked at her, without a word, and began to place his shirts and underwear in the empty chest on the wall next to the window.

"I've saved you the top drawer," he said.

While they were unpacking, Grace walked back into the living room where Richard was still napping, leaning even further on his side now. She put her hand on his forehead almost by instinct. What would it tell her, she wondered, and what would she do about it if she felt some unnatural warmth or chill?

He stirred and peered up at her.

"Is there something?" he mumbled.

"Deck's here with some girl."

"I was dreaming," he said. "That none of this is happening. Strange. What's she like?"

"I only just met her, Richard!"

"But you have an impression, don't you?"

"Well, I guess so," she said: "Perky."

"What does that mean?"

"Well, she was trying very hard to be pleasant. I don't know. *Perky*. The word just came to me. Seems to be nice looking enough. Brown hair. Good clothes. What does it matter? Do you want me to help you sit up?"

"Yes, and get me a drink, won't you? Something strong."

"It's awfully early, isn't it?" she said, reaching down and pulling him up gently.

"More like too late," he said, closing his eyes so that he wouldn't see her reaction.

When he heard her leave the room, he turned his head to look out toward the lake, across the lawn and toward the wooden dock. He could barely make out the boat bobbing gently at its mooring. The sun was higher now and the air would be warming outside, a deceitful warmth, however, because the nights were becoming almost icy, and a damp frost might still be trapped in the earth so that if you walked on it, it would give off a bitter sigh of cold, like an invisible spurt of fog. If they were to row out tomorrow as he planned, it would need to be early before the wind came up or the light fell behind the filter of the pine trees at the other end of the shore and the chill set in again.

He wasn't sure why he had insisted on taking his sons fishing. He knew it would be a terrible strain for him. Perhaps more than he should attempt. And everyone would object that he was too ill and feeble, as if he wasn't aware of that. But he had decided. Maybe it was the memory of much earlier times, when the boys were younger and they still looked up to him—at least when he thought they did—when they were together on some venture. Grace always said he refused to let them be themselves around him, and that he confined each of them to some prefigured role. But he had formed an impression of each when they were very young, and sometimes felt he knew them better than they knew themselves. It would have been hard to change that impression, even if he had wanted to. But he was sure he was right about them. Always had been.

He closed his eyes for a moment and then opened them again when he heard someone approach.

"Hello, Dad," Deck said. "How are you feeling?"

He looked up at his son, staring at him. It was the same Deck: the same eager, hungry eyes that seemed to lay claim to everything they lighted on. Of course he hadn't changed much since his last visit. A few extra pounds, but he kept himself in reasonably good shape. But what did he expect? And a different girl in tow again, as far as he could determine. He couldn't remember the name of the last one.

"So you've arrived," he said finally. "And who is this?"

"Susan."

"Hello, Mr. Collins," she said. "I'm Susan Barone. You have a lovely house, and the lake is just wonderful."

Richard looked up at her, nodded, but said nothing.

"It's so nice of you..."

"Have you seen your mother anywhere?" Richard interrupted, ignoring her. "I sent her on an errand. Couldn't have been that complicated."

Susan was about to continue, but Deck squeezed her hand so hard that she turned to look at him. It was as if he had intuited her next words, what she planned to say before she, herself, knew. But what, she wondered, was appropriate to say to someone you have just met and who is so visibly ill? How did you commiserate with them without pity? Or maybe the look of recognition on her face, her obvious shock at seeing his condition, was empathy enough. At that moment, she realized that she should be angry at Deck for dragging her into this fraught situation. Of course, he had explained the purpose of their visit, and he warned her that his father was gravely ill. But the words had sounded abstract and distant when he explained everything, and perhaps she wasn't really listening because she wanted the trip to be about something else. And now, confronting the actual situation and anticipating what the weekend was going to be like, she had to remind herself of why she had agreed. She had convinced herself that this was a test and a trial run of sorts that would inevitably come sooner or later in any serious relationship. But had they actually approached that point, she wondered? What was she doing, standing in this alien place where she was sure she didn't belong, staring down at a withered old man with a flushed face and knobby, blue-veined hands, who, nonetheless, seemed to command the room despite his infirmity?

"I have your drink," Grace said, approaching, as she broke into the silence that had followed Richard's question. "I'm sorry it took so long, but I thought I heard another car come up the road, and maybe it was Nick arriving. But not yet."

"Just put it down on the table, will you, Grace? And sit down all of you. You've got an old man at a disadvantage standing around looking at me like this is some sort of emergency room consultation."

"Oh Richard," Grace said. "You!"

"And Susan," he continued, finally recognizing her: "You're surely welcome here. It's always a pleasure to have such a good looking young woman around this house of decrepits."

He sat up straighter, without glancing at his wife, and leaned over to pick up his drink. He was determined to hold it without shaking, but when he grasped it and brought it up toward his mouth, his hand quivered violently, and the liquid spilled down the front of his shirt.

"Oh Richard, dear. Let me get a paper towel," Grace said, standing up abruptly. "Just put the glass down and I'll be right back."

He scowled at her as she scurried from the room, and then, squeezing his fist tightly, he brought the glass up to his mouth and quickly drank what remained, the cold ice cubes pressing against his lips. The sharp taste of the alcohol and the chill of the ice almost made him shudder with a momentary delight. At least, he thought, I can still feel something. And then he looked at Deck and Susan who were both trying to appear calm. He could almost read the strain on their faces, and it made him aware of how much they would scrutinize him for signs and the visible signals of his infirmities and his weaknesses. He was tempted to say something, to excuse himself, perhaps, or make a joke about dying. But it was what it was, and there was no point in trying to hide what they could so obviously see.

Grace rushed back from the kitchen with a clutch of paper towels in her hand and began to wipe the front of his shirt where the liquid had soaked through.

"Just hold still for a minute. And I'll get you a change of clothes."

"Don't bother, Grace," he said, pushing her away. "Damn you! Stop it! And quit hovering. It's OK. I'm really OK. Just sit down and stop scampering around! It's nothing. Just a spilled drink and not the end of the world."

"But..." she started to say, and then stopped. "Do you hear? I think that's a car door slamming. I'm sure it must be Nick."

She turned away and headed quickly into the kitchen and opened the back door.

"Yes," she called back. "I'm sure it's him!"

Deck looked at his father and then back to Susan. "Come on, Dad," he said, finally. "Mom's just trying to help."

His father said nothing because the words of justification died before he could utter them.

Grace opened the back door and stepped out onto the driveway, watching as her youngest son emerged from behind the upraised trunk of the car, carrying his suitcase. He waved with his free hand and then said something to the Uber driver who slammed the lid shut and then walked around to the driver's seat and began to back out.

"Mom," he called as he approached her. "It's wonderful to see you... but I'm so sorry. How is he doing?"

He embraced her, and then said nervously, "I'm sorry. I must smell like a long bus and train ride."

"Only like my grown up boy. That's all," she said, and then stopped, a look of disappointment flashed across her face: "You didn't bring your cello."

"No Mom, I just couldn't imagine it was a time for music."

"Well," she said. "Anyway. Come on in. Deck's already here—with a new girl, Susan something or other." She stopped and put her hand on his shoulder: "But I should warn you: your father looks terrible. I don't think he's suffering physically so much, but I think he's really afraid, and he snaps at everyone. Just so you'll know."

"I guess I'm ready for anything," he said. "But how are you, Mom? Are you holding up OK? It must be very hard."

"I suppose it is," she said. "He's changed—or maybe another self has emerged that was always inside him. Someone I haven't seen before. But I'm guessing it's just another phase of what I signed on for—that paragraph written in invisible ink on the other side of the wedding license and something the preacher never mentions."

"Oh, Mom! What a thing to say!" he said, hugging her again. He picked up his suitcase and followed her inside.

"You know where to put your things, don't you?"

"Sure; just give me a minute. I'm not quite ready to see him yet," he said and headed through the kitchen into the hallway and then to the bedroom. Once inside, he shut the door and hefted his suitcase onto the bed. It seemed strange to him that this room reflected none of his character, although he always stayed in it on every trip since his parents bought the house. It was a guest room with nondescript furnishings—all-gender and ambivalent, he thought with amusement: the way everything at his college was becoming.

For a few minutes, he could imagine himself to be a guest unpacking his things in a hotel room until he joined the rest of them, and then he would take his place as the second son—the artistic one, to use his father's favorite sarcastic euphemism. He was certain that despite the strained atmosphere around his father's condition and all the changes it implied, he, Nick, would gradually fall back into his other self, his younger being, and not the person that they didn't know, and that he was loath to reveal to them. And then he corrected himself: third son. There was always Seth. How could he forget Seth?

For some reason, at that moment, as he was putting his socks in the familiar dresser, the famous line of Tolstoy's flickered in his mind: something about unhappy families. He had even forgotten the name of the novel it came from. But he thought he'd want to amend that aphorism, whatever it said exactly. In his own experience, it was probably more on the mark to say, "*Every unhappy family is permanent in its own way.*" You couldn't escape who you had been and what their expectations were for you. No, they would never let you. You were always trapped in your past self whenever you were around your parents.

After he had unpacked the rest of his clothes and hung up a suit—something he brought along because he thought that his mother might insist on some formal dress—he changed his shirt and then headed out to the living room. All the while he had remained in the bedroom, he could hear the hesitant murmur of conversation, stopping and starting in the way a gathering of casual strangers might be searching for some common interest.

"Oh well," he said to himself.

They were all seated in a semi-circle around the couch when he entered the room. He walked quickly over to where his father sat and reached down to shake hands with him.

"Dad," he said, and then leaned back, surprised at how soft and cool his father's hand felt. He wasn't sure what to say next; surely not to comment on his pallor or the vivid red blotches on his cheeks. And so he turned around to greet his brother.

"It's been a while, hasn't it, Deck? Since last time we were all here—whenever that was," he said.

Deck smiled, gave him a chest bump and started to pull away, but Nick put his arms around his brother and hugged him tightly.

"Do I feel a few extra pounds?" he laughed.

"Pure muscle," Deck replied. And then, standing apart, he continued: "This is Susan. Meet my brother, the famous musician."

"Oh really?" she said enthusiastically. "What do you play?"

"Cello, primarily, but I actually teach all the stringed instruments."

"Oh, that's my favorite," she said. "Did you bring it along? It's such a lovely sound—so sad. I sometimes want to cry when I hear it. I'd love to hear you play."

"No," he said, looking at his father as if expecting some reaction. But he remained quietly staring at his sons.

"We'll eat in a few minutes. I don't suppose Seth will be here before late," his mother said.

"I notice that Dad has a drink," Deck interrupted. "Have you forgotten to ask us if we might want one? That long drive brings on a thirst, you know, and I could do with something strong. You too, Susan?"

"Well, yes, if everyone is having something. I think I will," she said.

As his mother was leaving the room, Nick called after her: "I'll have a beer if you have one, Mom. But let me help you. You want another one, Dad?"

His father, who seemed not to be listening, his head hanging at an odd angle, just nodded.

Standing in the kitchen with his mother, Nick watched her choking back tears.

"He doesn't focus all the time," she said. "You'll have to repeat yourself if you want his attention. And louder too."

"Is he really bad?"

"Yes. The doctor says it could be any day. The last heart attack really damaged him. I do wish he wouldn't drink, though."

"Does it matter?"

"No. I suppose not."

"Does he know?"

"Yes. More than that. I think he's prepared. But you'd think that feeling so bad and being sick and weak and all would allow him to put all his legal fixations aside. What I mean is that he still tries to be precise about everything—he's so abrupt and dogmatic—ready to enter an objection to the things I say or do when I try to help him. I guess he's trying to cling onto something—not so much life as it is now—but the life he had."

"Good old Dad. Lawyer, judge, prosecutor, and supreme

court justice combined. But you don't expect him to change at this late stage, do you? I guess it's good to hang on that way."

"Oh, Nick," she sobbed suddenly. "It's so terrible, and I've been so lonely. You don't know what it's like being with someone who..."

"It's OK, Mom. We're here for you now."

"With someone," she continued, "who seems so determined to make *everyone* miserable and just as unhappy as he is."

"Is there something else? What do you mean?"

"He'll tell you. Yes. He'll tell you."

"Is this some kind of mystery, Mom? Should I prepare myself?"

"Yes, you should," she said, and then turned away from him to reach up for glasses in the top of the cupboard. He thought, however, that she wanted to hide the tears that he noticed were beginning to creep around the corners of her eyes.

"I'll pour three whiskeys," she said, still facing away from him. "You can get some ice from the refrigerator and take a beer if you want. I think there are two or three there. The kind you like."

"Anything will be fine," he said.

When they had finished their drinks, everyone started for the dining room,

"Can I help you, Dad?" Deck asked, reaching down to pull his father up.

Richard just grimaced, as if his response was stuck inside him but allowed his son to help.

The table was set for seven, with two empty chairs. Susan sat at the opposite end next to Grace, and the rest of the family took their accustomed places.

"Just like it always was," Deck said.

"Except that your brother hasn't arrived yet," his father said, gesturing weakly toward the two vacant chairs. "Always the last one. And inconsiderate to the end."

"Well I, for one, give thanks for that," Deck blurted out. "I'm already exhausted from hearing his stories, and he hasn't even started one yet!" He didn't add that the worst part would be his father's interruptions.

Nick said nothing, but he also felt mildly relieved. As soon as Seth arrived, all the old tensions would burst out again, like the sudden explosion of heat when dry kindling catches fire. And he wondered if his father, in his condition, would be up to the challenge. Or would he be that changed? Would any of them ever be changed?

Susan was puzzled by this brief exchange about the missing brother, and she looked quizzically at Deck. But he shook his head slowly, and she didn't ask the question that she intended. This absent brother was a mystery, and she was curious about someone who seemed to provoke such strong opinions. This was a strange family, she decided, all of them speaking in a coded language that she didn't understand. All the more reason to be careful about what she said.

CHAPTER 7

It was around midnight when Seth and Lee arrived, coasting their camper carefully into the driveway as silently as possible. Grace had left the back door unlocked so they could slip in, but she was waiting for them in the darkened living room. Everyone else had gone to bed. A lemon slice of moon had long since passed above the tops of the pines and disappeared over the house, but, in this deserted spot, without ambient lights, its glow was just enough to create shadows and patches of silver on the lawn and polish the soft waves of the lake with hints of light and muted gold. She knew that if she walked outside, she would leave glistening footprints on the damp grass—transient marks that would melt away at dawn. So impermanent and final, like... she thought. And then she refused the next idea that came to her—shaking her head at the sad, insistent logic of her musing, this melancholy declension of her grief.

"Hi, Mom," Seth said quietly as he crept into the living room. "I was pretty sure you'd stay up. And thanks for leaving the back door open."

"Seth!" she exclaimed quietly, standing and hugging him.

"Lee is still in the camper. I just wanted to say hello—and let you know that we've arrived. So now you can go to bed."

"I'm so happy you're here Seth. With all the others."

"Yes, Mom. We're here. I'll just slip outside again. See you in the morning. Bright and early."

The next day was already warm and overcast, with a moist wind blowing out of the south and gently shaking the trees around the house. Grace was up at dawn, but when she entered the kitchen, her daughter-in-law was busy making a large pot of coffee.

"I didn't know what else to do, Mother," Lee said. "I looked in the refrigerator, and there's lots for a breakfast, but I didn't want to start—I know that you got everything planned."

Grace looked at her and almost spoke in anger. She hated to be called *Mother*. It just sounded wrong to her and foreign and stilted from someone she scarcely knew. But she said nothing. Perhaps she should talk to Seth—tell him that it wasn't right. But both of them, and Seth particularly, were so strange, and she wondered if it was their religion that enthralled them both in peculiarity. She never would have believed that her big-hearted, clumsy son could become such a fervent believer and someone who was never bashful about injecting religion into every conversation now. There was nothing in his past to explain this. She and Richard had never been religious in any meaningful way, at least since they were very young. Church was just a social obligation for them now. On those rare occasions when she had gone to a service, she still enjoyed the music and the hour of shared intimacy with people she only knew by sight. The best part of it reminded her of her childhood, when Sunday was a day where everyone dressed up in their best and, after church, visited old aunts and uncles who always had a lemonade cookie or some sweet to offer her. And how she had loved the shine and elegance of the patent leather shoes her mother had bought her, and the way they almost danced on her feet! But that was so long ago, a lifetime once removed, and a faded childhood memory. And ever since she and Richard had settled by the lake, church had become just another building they passed on the way into town and of no particular obligation.

Except there was that one time, a few days after Richard had his first heart attack, when she had ventured into the local Methodist church to speak to the minister. She wasn't sure what she wanted from him—comfort, perhaps, or reassurance. She had acted on a childish instinct—she realized that now. And she had left his office discouraged listening to his platitudes, and never returned. How was it then that her son had become so zealous, she wondered? She was sure it was Lee who had convinced him. Maybe that was for the best, even if she didn't understand. He certainly was changed—*tamed*, was the right word, she thought.

The two women worked together silently, preparing breakfast. Lee set the table in the dining room, and gradually, everyone but Richard appeared. They ate quickly, with little conversation, and left the table as soon as they finished. Only Seth remained.

"I'll need to get Richard up now," Grace announced, wiping her hands on a dish towel after she had cleared the table. "He's difficult in the morning."

"I'll help," Seth said, standing quickly.

"All right, yes," Grace said, "but you should be aware that he tries to do everything himself—even though he can't. He gets so angry if I say anything. So just pretend like you're not lifting him up or putting on his socks." She didn't add that his illness had made their lives a game of charades and pretenses. It would be much too cynical to admit that, even if it was the truth.

While everyone had been eating breakfast, Richard lay half awake, waiting for someone to come. When he was by himself like this, when he could hear the murmur of conversations and then some sudden exclamation, he felt more alone and isolated than ever. Since his first heart attack, he and Grace had slept in separate beds, and he hated the isolation. Neither of them had ever said much about it, but now he thought it had been a kind of premonition of dying, when the warmth they had once shared had become a frustration to their sleep. They had grown apart, he thought, in this long marriage of theirs. They had loved each other once, at least he thought so. But now she had become his distorting mirror, and he couldn't bear to see his fate in the worry lines on her face, or the loose flesh around her jaws, and the mottled skin that her efforts to hide under makeup still failed to disguise. Yes, he knew he was dying, and yet he couldn't tell what it was that he felt—nervous impatience waiting for it to happen, wanting to get it over with, or some terrible dread that made him gasp. But when he thought of it, he tried to hold his breath, and his whole body tingled with anxious anticipation. No matter how he tried, the thought was larger than anything else.

Seth entered the darkened room where Richard lay and immediately walked over to pull aside the curtains.

"Hello, Dad. I'm here to get you up," he said, looking down at his father. "It's a bit cloudy so far today, but I'm hoping that the sun is going to shine later on. Try to sit up and I'll help you stand."

Richard leaned forward so his son could put his arms around him. It embarrassed him to be embraced this way, but he didn't protest. It was better than the stumbling efforts of his wife in the morning.

"Just relax," Seth said, surprised that the dead weight of this body could feel so brittle at the same time. "Don't want to hurt you."

"Wouldn't matter, Son."

"Of course it matters, Dad. No need to speed up God's plan for you by injuring you."

"God doesn't have a plan for me or anyone else," Richard protested weakly.

Seth said nothing, but it troubled him that his father was so hostile to the truth, especially now in his last days. It had impressed him deeply when he witnessed members of his congregation greet the coming of the end with jubilant expectation and hope. Expressing none of the misery he could immediately sense in this moment with his father. If only he could persuade him to accept the joy that he had come to realize. It would ease the tension that was almost palpable in the air of the house, a fog of emotion and fear that seemed to make everyone appear indistinct and half visible, like wavering souls wandering aimlessly through a thick haze of apprehension. Not knowing the way.

When Richard was finally dressed, Seth left him in the bathroom, leaning against the sink, trying to shave as best he could.

This was going to be a special day when he would tell them all of his plan, Richard thought, and he needed to appear strong and in control of himself. The way he had always been. But looking in the mirror at the patches of shaving cream that still clung to his lank cheeks, he knew that, on the contrary, he appeared weak and pale. The whites of his eyes had a yellow tinge with a filigree of red blood vessels reaching out from the edges. He blinked in disgust at the sight. Reaching down, he splashed warm water from the faucet on his face, wiped his jaw with a towel, and eased his way out. Seth stood in the hall, waiting to take him into the dining room.

"I can walk," he said, almost angrily. "Just give me your arm."

Seth held out his elbow and the two shuffled slowly down the hall toward the dining room, where one place was still set.

Richard ate carefully, but only a single piece of toast, which he could hold in his hand without shaking. He wasn't hungry; he hadn't been for several days. But he knew he needed strength for the task of this day. After that, perhaps, he might just stop for good.

One by one, the others in the house peered into the dining room, and he asked each of them to remain until they were all present.

It made him more resolute in his task to see them all sitting around the table, waiting for him to speak. A bit like it had always been. He was cautious about what he was going to say. But for a brief moment, he felt a swell of energy and excitement.

Indeed, he had a surprise for them, and it was certainly not at all what they expected.

"I'm happy to see all of you here," he said. "I know you've come a long way, and it's wonderful to have the whole family together again."

It took almost all his strength to continue, so he had to pause:

"And I know these are not happy circumstances. My condition isn't ever going to improve. But enough of that. I want to tell you—Deck, Seth, and Nick—that I have a little fishing expedition planned for us today. We'll take the boat out on the lake later this morning when the weather improves a bit."

He was pleased to see the look of surprise on their faces.

"Please, Richard," Grace said, half standing up. "Don't even think about going out on that boat."

"Do you think I'm not up to it?" he said.

"It's a terrible idea," she replied. "I can't imagine anything worse."

"Well, if you're worried that one of your sons will fall into the lake, remember that they are all pretty good swimmers."

"You old fool," she laughed nervously. "You know I'm only worried about you."

"Of course I know," he said, "and I intend to catch more than the three of them combined. They never could compete with me."

"Are you sure you want to do this?" Deck asked. "Isn't it dangerous? All that physical effort."

"I'd rather die doing something I enjoy than sitting around this damned house in my bathrobe and slippers with you characters sobbing over me. No, I've decided."

"Great idea, Dad," Seth said. "Reminds me of the time

you took us up to Canada on that trip. Do you remember?"

"Yes," he answered warily.

"Nick was just a tiny tyke of a kid, and Deck must have been what, around twelve or so?"

"I think so."

"And what about that fish I caught? A northern pike. You remember? Must have been two feet long, and what a fighter!"

"I remember a fish, Seth, but certainly not that size."

"Oh, I'm sure it was. Don't you remember what our Indian guide said when I finally hauled it up to the side of the boat?"

"It wasn't that big, Son. No reason to exaggerate. Don't start...."

"But everyone thought it was. Aren't I right, Deck? You remember don't you?"

"I remember fishing, vaguely," Deck replied.

"It was huge. I told you about it didn't I, Lee?"

"Stop it! Just stop it!" his mother interrupted. "I can't bear it. Stop!"

There was a sudden, uncomfortable silence, as if she had willed a vacuum.

Susan looked nervously around the room, but avoided Deck's eyes. She felt she had to say something.

"I've always wondered why they call it a school of fish," she said after a minute. "I've always wondered."

"Because fish swim in rows, like students in a classroom," Deck said, dismissively.

"The other day," Susan continued, ignoring him, her voice stronger now that she had their attention,

"On the web, I looked up all the names for groups of animals. I don't know why I did it. Just for fun, I suppose.

You know: Like a 'pride of lions.' I'd heard that one lots of times before. But there are such strange ones. Like a 'coalition of cheetahs' and an 'intrusion of cockroaches.' I get that one, I guess. But what about a 'horde of gerbils'? Isn't that the silliest thing you ever heard?"

Deck gave her a look that said, "enough," but she appeared not to see him.

"And what about a 'troubling of goldfish'? That's all I can remember, but I wish I had written down some of the others."

She hesitated. And then Deck said, looking straight at his father, "Did you find any names for a group of attorneys? If not, I could suggest some."

"Deck! Don't," his mother said.

"How about a '*corruption of lawyers*'?" he continued, not sure why his father suddenly made him angry. But he persisted, as if his own hostility was contagious: "Or maybe '*a contempt of attorneys*'? I'll bet you'd find that on the web somewhere. If not, there ought to be."

"I don't know, probably," his father said, faintly. "But maybe you'd find '*an ingratitude of sons*' somewhere."

"Oh, please stop it. Stop it, Both of you!" Grace cried. "You're not being funny, you two!"

Without another word, she hurried out of the room and headed immediately to the bedroom. Without really being conscious of what she was doing, she straightened the sheets on Richard's bed and moved mechanically around the room, touching the curtains on the window, as if they needed straightening, running her finger across the top of the dresser to check for dust, and then stooping to pick up a bit of paper that had fallen on the floor. Why had such bitterness fallen on the family—and especially now? Why did Deck resent his father so much? And silent Nick—quiet and keeping his secrets. She could almost read their thoughts. It was as if they had a premonition of the terrible and unfair thing he planned to do—she couldn't help thinking about it. It had hung over her like a precariously balanced evil ever since he announced it to her. And now she thought—even worse—that his plan somehow implied a truth about their marriage and perhaps even a revelation about their lives together and the family they had created—as if somehow it was her fault. He had always treasured the law, and she had forever refused to admit to herself that legal matters actually came first in his affection. But ever since he retired, she could sense his unhappiness and frustration. It was almost as if he had lost a lover, someone so dear to him that their absence had carved out of him some part of his very essence, leaving him to be just the hollow, bitter remnant of himself—the part of him that was left for her. And she was not enough.

When she first realized his frustration, she had felt an enormous sympathy for him—losing his life's work had been a terrible thing. She understood that. But it gradually became apparent to her that her own role in his life must have been like a convenient mistress, almost like a pathetic supplicant for whatever occasional affection he might muster. She had been more like a comfortable habit than anything! Perhaps she had allowed herself to recognize this fact before, whenever she felt particularly lonely. But she had always dismissed the idea as self-indulgent. But now, in these last few months, when he had weakened and become more dependent on her, she had gained the strength to think back and reconsider their lives together. Odd, she thought, that only when her own energy surpassed his could she allow herself to examine old, suppressed feelings, almost as if she had discovered an old, yellowed photograph and was seeing faces that were familiar but now looked like antiquated parodies of themselves.

And as for his sons, their sons: of course, he had been present in their lives in a conventional way, and she had always considered his strictness to be a semblance of love. Maybe it was: and the only way he knew how. But now she wondered, if it came down to it, what he really felt about them. Had fatherhood always been an obligation without much passion? And she had to ask herself if he had ever experienced the almost painful swell of pride in his sons that she always felt when she looked at them. It didn't matter to her what they accomplished or did or didn't do; they were hers. Even Seth. But she had no idea what Richard felt, and especially now.

She sat down abruptly on his unmade bed and put her head on the covers. His smell was faint but still present, and she leaned up on an elbow and punched his pillow hard, twice, with her other hand to stop herself from sobbing. She had become so angry with him, so furious that he was ill and dying! Everything she had been thinking just now had to be wrong or a terrible exaggeration; she knew that. It wouldn't surprise her that she was just creating a caricature of him to avoid her pain, creating someone hateful so she could distance herself from him and allow him to slip out of her life. But she knew that whatever he was or had been, he continued to be an essential part of her being. Something would die in her when he was gone. It was dangerous to feel sorry for yourself because then everything you saw and heard was a distortion, she thought. But she couldn't help herself. She still loved him. She always would, no matter what.

She sat up, and then stood, bracing herself against the wooden headboard. This was no time to imagine herself alone; those days would come later—inevitably and unwelcome and too soon. She needed to face up to today. That was enough.

Straightening the bed covers, she left the bedroom and returned to the living room where everyone was sitting, watching her silently as if they expected to see some great transformation in her.

"I was just making the bed," she explained, trying to dominate the emotion in her voice. She understood that Richard was determined to take his sons fishing, and that any further objection on her part would just seem to be whining.

"While you men folks are out on the lake," she continued, trying to sound chipper, "we three, Lee and Susan and I, will have a nice cup of tea in the kitchen, a nice get-together, and maybe cook up something surprising for lunch. I'm sure you'll all be hungry when you get back."

"Maybe we'll catch a fish or two," Nick said, trying to sound enthusiastic about something he dreaded doing.

"I wouldn't count on it," Deck said, "unless, of course, Dad is lucky. Like he usually is," he added. "Or maybe Seth will catch another whale!"

"I'm all for it," Seth exclaimed. "What are we going for? Bluegills? Small mouth bass?"

"The tackle box and rods are in the garage," Richard said, "why don't you get them out, Nick? And if one of you others could just help me up, I'll try to make my way down to the dock."

"Lean on me, Dad," Seth said, moving over quickly to help him.

"That's OK. Deck can do it. Now let's get moving. Fish tend to bite early on in my experience," he said, surprised that he felt a sudden rush of vigor. The doctor had said this might happen—that there might be times when he felt his energy returning—but he had cautioned that these moments would only be temporary and dangerous, and he should be careful not to exert himself too much.

"Exuberance can be deadly," he had warned. But Richard didn't pay any attention because he understood that the doctor was just looking over his shoulder at a possible lawsuit. He, of all patients, understood the way the threat of medical malpractice hung over the head of every diagnosis.

While they had been sitting in the living room, with conversations buzzing around him, he had been preoccupied by the excitement and anticipation he felt, because he could only think that this outing had a much more serious purpose than catching a fish or two. He planned to speak to his sons away from the house, away from Grace, who would be so disapproving when he finally told them, and away from Seth's wife and that other woman who might not understand the serious intent of what he was going to do—who would certainly misunderstand and might be appalled at his motives. He wanted to state his intentions clearly, and make his sons understand that he was doing it for them, and he could not do that with an audience listening in like an unsworn panel of jurists.

Deck walked over, grabbed his father under the arms, and pulled him upright out of his chair. He then guided him slowly out of the living room, out the sliding glass door, onto the deck and then to the wooden steps that led down into the garden and toward the lake. It was the first time in several weeks that Richard had approached the dock where the boat was tethered. It was probably a mistake to leave it in the water for such a prolonged time, but he had always thought, always yearned, to climb into it when his health improved. That was a false expectation, of course, and he knew it, but the sight of it bobbing gently on the waves seemed to signal hope, and so long as it remained there, the seats empty but inviting, he could anticipate rowing out onto the lake. And now it was going to happen, even if this would be the very last time.

Seth, Deck, and Richard waited on the dock for Nick to fetch the fishing tackle from the garage. The air was soft but still slightly chilly and an ineffective sun just made the atmosphere visibly dense through the low clouds. Off in the distance, the jagged outline of the pine trees stood as if they rose from the dark water itself. There were only a few waves that jostled the boat, touching its edge against the soft round buoys that hung over the side of the dock. On a bright day, there might be herons standing motionless on one leg among the congregation of tall cattails grouped on the west side of the lake, their beaks and eyes cast in a downward trance. Waiting. And if the boat approached too close to their positions, they would squawk in protest against the intrusion and struggle reluctantly up into the air, with the audible beat of their heavy wings. If it was truly a good day for catching fish, there would be bright sunlight to attract dragonflies that skimmed the surface of the water, in double jeopardy from the jaws of a jumping fish or the sharp beak of a swooping swallow. And perhaps there would be the raucous skid of a pair of ducks landing.

But today, as Richard looked out over the expanse, there was almost no motion, and all that was alive seemed hidden and waiting.

"I think I found everything," Nick called out as he approached the men standing on the dock. "I've got several rods and reels and there was a tin box that seems to have some flies and artificial worms in it. I looked inside. I hope that's all you meant."

"Good enough, son," Richard said. "Now let's get into the boat and shove off. Fish are waiting."

Deck, who was still clutching his father's arm, edged him over to the side of the boat, while Seth climbed in to steady him. When they were both seated, Nick set the rods and tackle box in an empty space at the front of the boat and stepped on the bench beside them. As he did, the boat rocked dangerously, and a small tongue of water lapped over the edge, pooling at the bottom of the hull.

"Be careful, Nick!" Richard exclaimed, knowing full well that his warning had come too late. But he wanted to remind them that standing up in the boat made it particularly unsteady. "You can cast off now if you're sitting down," he continued. "Just unloop that rope from around the post." Turning, he called to the back, "And you, Deck, do the same to the rope at your end. And then you can row us out into the middle. Just be careful not to hit anyone with the oars."

Deck glanced at his father and then turned away so that he wouldn't see the annoyance on his face. Before, when he was younger, he would have deeply resented instructions to perform the obvious. He might even have protested. But under the circumstances he could almost forgive the fussiness of his father; it was better just to ignore him.

When they reached the middle of the lake, Richard asked Deck to stop. They could drift in any direction; it didn't matter because, he said, the best fishing would be to cast toward the shore. For the next few minutes, they passed rods around and baited their hooks. Seth was the first to finish, and he stood up and threw his line twenty feet toward the stand of cattails, rocking the boat as he did.

"Be careful, damn it!" Deck shouted. "You'll pitch us all into the water if you don't watch out."

"That's all right," Seth laughed. "I'm always ready to save you, brother, when you're falling into the deep."

"Some reassurance," Deck said, disgusted because he was sure that Seth was preaching at him. "Yeah, like you've always been there to catch me." He said this hoping that his brother would hear the sarcasm in his voice. There were times when Seth infuriated him, and he hoped he realized it.

Nick just looked at his two brothers, and then stared at his father, who had a very strange expression on his face. He couldn't determine if it was a sudden wave of pain or anguish or expectation, but his eyes were intense, and the hand holding his fishing rod was trembling. He had the sudden, awful premonition (no—knowledge!) that this was the last time he would ever see his father, and he didn't want to remember him this way—as a shrunken version of himself, without the strength or the energy that he had sometimes admired and always feared.

Neither he nor Seth had inherited his father's absolute determination and drive, and he had to admit, both of them had, in their own peculiar ways, drifted into a stunted adulthood. He had settled into a mediocre career in the "Unnecessary University," as he liked to call it. And there was Deck—yes, even Deck—the successful brother, if you counted on money alone, but whose relationships always seemed to end in failure. Only Seth seemed happy and Nick was almost jealous of the strange life he led, even though he couldn't imagine it.

Deck was the first one of them to remark on the thunder sounding off in the distance, and the darkening cloud rising up to the north, although they all must have noticed.

"I suppose we ought to go back now," he said, "in case it's a real storm brewing."

"Not likely this time of year," his father said. "But we can stop fishing for a minute. No luck anyway."

"Shall I row back to the dock?" Deck asked, reaching down for the oars.

"No, not quite yet," his father said. "There's something I need to tell you boys."

CHAPTER 8

A sudden breeze caught the back door of the kitchen and swung it shut.

"It looks like it might rain," Grace said, standing up from the table where they sat to look out the window. It was an empty gesture because she knew she wouldn't be able to see anything except the back yard and the driveway where Seth's camper was parked and maybe a darkening sky over the tops of the trees. But she was nervous, worrying about Richard and uncomfortable sitting and just doing nothing.

Returning to the table in the middle of the room, she asked: "Would either of you like more tea? Lee? Susan? I can heat up some water. I'm sorry I don't have any cake or biscuits. What with..."

"Don't bother, Mother," Lee said. "This is fine. We understand."

She sat down and picked up her cup, although she knew it just contained a residue of cold liquid.

No one said anything for a moment. They could have been strangers, Grace thought; in fact they were, in a way: brought together by tenuous family ties, or was it by some vague anticipation to be witnesses to a ritual?

Susan shifted her weight in the uncomfortable wooden chair. She knew she was out of place, and it made her determined to say something. It was disconcerting just to sit. But what?

"I'm curious about where you come from, Lee?" she said finally.

"Florida," Lee said, smiling. "Seth and I, we drove up outa' Florida."

Susan looked surprised for a moment: "No," she said, "I mean really. Where do you really come from?"

"Well, St. Louis, originally."

Susan looked exasperated, and she felt, for a moment, that Lee was mocking her, refusing to admit that she was some sort of immigrant. It was just conversation, and she was bored and trying to say just anything, not hold an inquisition.

Lee looked at her and then laughed: "Korea. That's where I grown up. Osan. A city you probably never heard about."

"Why did you say St. Louis, then? I don't understand."

"It's where I met Seth and where I found God. Before that, well, I just wasn't myself. My real life began there. And here in America."

Susan looked down at her cup and then back to Lee.

"If you don't mind, I'm curious. What kind of religion is that, then?"

Grace suddenly wanted to intervene. It wasn't right of Susan to pry. But before she could say anything, Lee continued:

"I'm a Witness, and Seth is too."

Susan hesitated for a moment, and then asked:

"Jehovah Witness or whatever? Does that mean you go around and knock on doors?"

"Sometimes," Lee said. "It's our obligation to share our joyfulness."

"I think we should begin to make lunch for the men... when they get back," Grace said quietly, embarrassed at the talk about religion.

"Won't we be cooking fish?" Susan asked.

"They aren't really fishing," Grace said abruptly.

"I don't understand," Susan said. "Why go out in a boat then? Especially if it looks like rain?"

"I think Richard wanted to be alone with his sons. And away from us. To tell them something."

"Something that we shouldn't hear?" Susan asked.

"Yes," Grace said.

There was quiet in the room, and Grace wanted to get up again and peer out the window, but she remained in her chair.

"Don't you believe in anything, Susan?" Lee asked.

"Sure. I'm a Catholic. Not that I go to Mass anymore. Who does? But I was raised that way."

Grace stood and walked over to the refrigerator. She couldn't help herself; she had to be doing something. Lee and Susan were making her nervous. And the talk of religion.

"I'll get a few things out. You girls can set the table in a minute if you will," she said.

"Sit down, Mother," Lee exclaimed. "I'll do everything. Just tell me what."

"No, please. I want to do it."

"OK. I understand," Lee said. "But if there's anything..."

Grace swung the refrigerator door open and began

pulling out packages of lunch meat and cheeses, which she set on the counter next to the sink. She reached back inside again and grasped a bottle of juice. It almost slipped out of her hand, but she managed to put it on the table.

"Thank God that Richard didn't see that. He gets so upset, and I'm so clumsy sometimes," she exclaimed.

"Please let me help," Lee said. "Just sit down."

"All right," Grace said. "You can get the plates and dishes. They're up on the top shelf in the cabinet next to the stove. The ones with the gold rims. I haven't used them in ages, but I thought today... just for a change. They've been in my family for ages."

Lee got up and walked to the cabinet. Opening it, she reached up and placed several plates carefully on the table.

"Why these are beautiful!" she exclaimed. "Where are they from?"

"They were Mama's," Grace said. "They're almost the only thing I have left from her."

"They're lovely," Susan said, picking one up. "Is this porcelain?"

"Not exactly; it's bone china. You can see the light through it if you hold it up."

Susan picked up a plate and stared intently at it.

"And the gold around the edges. Is it real?" she asked.

"Yes," Grace said. "Someone in my family painted it on. I don't know who. It's gold leaf, so it can peel off if you wash it in really hot water. That's why I never take them out. It's just a memory, I guess. But today, for some reason I thought we'd use it tonight."

She looked at the stack of dishes and then put her arm up to cover her eyes.

Lee looked at her sadly: "Has it been bad? Are you all right?"

"Everything," she said quietly. "Everything is wrong."

Lee reached over and touched Grace's hand. "You'll be OK. Just trust in God."

Grace pulled her hand away. It was an automatic impulse, and she felt instantly ashamed of herself for rejecting a gesture that she knew to be well-intentioned. But when she looked at Lee, it almost made her angry to see the bland confidence on her face. Her contentment was even visible beneath her concern. How could she possibly know what was going to happen, or what was occurring on the boat out on the lake, or understand what it was like to live with Richard, and watch his disintegration and feel his anger and his despair? Long ago, she had fallen in love with his strength and determination, his honesty and forthrightness, but now she thought she almost hated him for his weakness. It occurred to her that the most tightly wound people are the ones who feel most in danger of coming apart. Perhaps that explained something about him. Perhaps that was why the law appealed to him, with its rigorous order and its abstract rules. And now, everything had changed, and there was nothing left for her (or him) to hang onto. And the thin reed of their affection had bent, and she had fallen down with him into a slough of despair.

She wondered how Lee could ever understand how she felt, living, as her daughter-in-law did, in a blinding fog of religious conviction, and never facing up to the awfulness that life could visit on you: the awfulness that Seth and his brothers were about to learn. She wondered if she should tell Lee what Richard intended just to make her understand. But she said nothing, knowing it would be wrong to involve Susan in this, too. It was wrong for her to be here in the first place. Deck was so inconsiderate, thinking only of himself. Why did he bring her? Everything seemed to be going wrong.

A sudden flash of lightning lit the room, followed by the distant boom of thunder.

Grace exclaimed: "I hope now they'll return as soon as they see that a storm is coming up."

"Why don't you go into the living room, Mother, and wait for them? Susan and I can finish in the kitchen," Lee said.

"No! And please stop calling me Mother," she said suddenly. "If you have to, I'm Grace. Please. And I'll finish with the lunch."

"Of course," Lee said. "I was only trying to help."

"I know. But you can't. It's the only thing I have left. It's the only purpose for me. I'm just not ready to let go yet."

But she did not say to them—these two accidental companions—that she was changing, and the circumstances of Richard's illness and his departing gestures were, in fact, forcing her to reconsider her own life and the decisions she had made. This was something that she thought should occur to you if you were seriously ill and had to contemplate the end. But, strangely, as she watched her husband trying to arrange his departure and leave life exactly as he wished it to be, it was happening to her, too.

Lee motioned to Susan, and the two of them walked out of the kitchen, through the dining room and into the living room. Lee went over to the window and looked out. She could see the small boat, outlined against the dark water, and the four men sitting in it. She could detect no movement, and it was too hazy to know if they were gesturing. She wondered why they didn't turn back to shore now that the storm was approaching.

Still in the kitchen, Grace was standing by the sink. She looked at the counter on her right, where she had stacked several plates. Next to them was a platter on which she had placed the cold cuts. She hadn't taken down glasses yet and the silverware drawer remained closed.

She started to open it and then hesitated. She suddenly felt an enormous fatigue, as if her body recognized what she was determined not to admit to herself: that she was tired—more tired than she had ever been. It occurred to her that her anger at Lee was just part of this denial. Good intentions could curdle into a sour disposition, and she now regretted the way she dismissed her daughter-in-law. It had been cruel and uncalled for.

She had refused to admit it, but she realized that she wanted help from Seth's wife, to be closer to her. Maybe it was because she had never had the daughter she wanted so much—the two daughters, in fact, that her miscarriages had denied her. Strange to think about all that now, after so many years had passed. But whenever Seth was present, she was reminded of those moments long before, and the time in the hospital room when she had held him instead of the infant she had wanted and expected.

She walked slowly over to the entrance to the dining room. She could see through it to where Susan and Lee were standing together, looking out the picture window toward the lake and the men in the boat.

"Lee," she called out. And then louder: "Lee, would you come into the kitchen for a moment?"

She turned around and waited.

Lee appeared a moment later, a quizzical look on her face.

"Did you want something, Grace?" she said.

"Mother," Grace said as she walked over and took Lee in her arms, holding her tight for a moment. "It's Mother; I want you to call me Mother, and please, could you help me set out the lunch?"

CHAPTER 9

Nick wondered if his father had brought them to the middle of the lake just for that reason—to be away from the women and together with his sons, or if there was another purpose hiding behind the fishing expedition.

"In fact, there are two things," Richard said, trying to hold back the tension he could feel, and not wanting to blurt out what needed to be said carefully and judiciously. He had waited for weeks to say this and, in his mind, he had rehearsed exactly how he would approach it and the words he would use. But now it seemed as if all that meticulous planning had escaped him, and for once he felt he was unable to master the emotion of the moment.

"I'm dying," he said. "You realize that, don't you? Your mother has probably told you everything. But the doctor said it could happen any time now. I wouldn't have asked you all here if it wasn't serious—I wanted to see you for the last time."

"Come on, Dad," Seth interrupted. "Only God can know that."

"Yes, and the doctor," Nick breathed.

"Don't interrupt me!" Richard said firmly. "I've accepted

my sentence, and I'm as prepared as anyone can be. And scared, I'll admit," he mumbled softly.

"But I want to tell you about my will," he continued.

Just then, there was a brief, bright flash of lightning, striking somewhere off in the distance, but close enough to momentarily light up their faces.

"We ought to turn back now," Deck said, starting to raise up the oars.

"No, not yet," his father said firmly. "I've got to finish now that I started," he paused to take a deep breath, and a wave of pain shot through his chest. But he ignored it and continued:

"I've made my will, and I want you to understand what it is and why I did it. You, Deck and Nick, will each get seven percent of my estate and Seth, you will receive three percent. The bulk of my estate will be held in trust for your mother. The proceeds will be distributed so that she can live a comfortable life."

He stopped for a moment to catch his breath. It had been a long time since he had spoken such fraught words, and it would take a serious effort to continue but he didn't want any stumble to distort his meaning before he finished.

"When your mother passes, her trust will revert to the University's new Law School here in town. They're going to rename it after me and there will be some fellowships for young men and women to make a career. There are a few other charities I have mentioned, but that's the gist of it."

Off in the near distance came the shallow hiss of rain as it began to sweep across the lake. No one said anything for a moment, but Deck looked at Nick, who seemed to be studying something on the floor of the boat.

"I think we need to go back right now," Seth said. "You mustn't get chilled, Dad, and the rain may get heavy."

"Are you serious, Dad?" Deck asked. "Is that why you brought us out here? Just to tell us? Is this your idea of drama? Four men trapped in a boat so you could watch our reaction?"

He didn't wait for an answer or move, except to replace the oars in their recess on the sides of the boat. He just sat still for a moment, letting the rain, which had reached them now, drain down his face.

"What about you, Nick? Just going to sit there with a stupid look on your face?"

"I don't know what to say," Nick replied.

"You never did!"

"And you, Seth?" Deck murmured. "You?"

"Give me the damn oars, Deck," Seth shouted. "If you won't row us back, I will!" He stood up, rocking the boat dangerously, and pushed Deck aside so he could grab the oars.

"Someone give Dad their shirt to put over his head."

No one moved until Nick finally pulled his t-shirt over his head and handed it to his father while Seth jerked the oars, pulling the boat rapidly through the water.

Fortunately, a wind had come up behind them and they quickly reached the dock. Deck climbed out immediately and began to head back to the house, but Seth shouted at him again:

"Help us, Deck, for God's sake! What do you think you're doing? Help him out while I tie the boat up."

Deck turned around, hesitated for a moment, and then returned to give his hand to Nick to pull him up onto the dock. Then the two of them reached for their father, who was standing in Seth's embrace.

A dark rain was now falling in torrents and lightning flashed nearer, momentarily revealing the swaying trees. All of them were soaked as they slowly made their way up the slippery lawn to the side entrance to the house. Grace and Lee stood at the open door, holding out towels that they handed to the men as they approached.

"Get Dad inside," Seth ordered. "He's really wet. I'll help you take his wet clothes off and get him into bed."

Richard felt himself handed around in the strong grip of his son. It was almost a pleasant sensation, although his heart was pounding. But he let himself be carried into the bedroom and was scarcely conscious when his son and wife stripped off his clothes, dried him off, and placed him gently in the bed. At any other time in his life he would have protested violently against this intimacy, but all he wanted now was to sink down and relax into someone else's strength.

As they pulled the covers up over him, he began to shiver, feeling as if he could not control the shaking that had taken sudden possession of his body. He glanced up at Grace and tried to speak. Words formed in his mind, but he was unable to force them out of his mouth. He had no breath, no energy. He thought he could hear someone talking, but whatever it was they were saying seemed to come from a great distance, the indistinct sounds fading in and out. He wanted to shout, to say that he was alive and he would be all right—that they should leave him alone, but he could not hear himself speak.

Grace put her hand on his forehead and pushed back the wisps of damp grey hair that were clinging to his brow.

He could feel the warmth of her palm, and he wanted to reach out from the covers and touch her, but he was unable to move his arms. He only knew that he was lying in his bed.

He could see them next to him, and they appeared to be moving, almost swaying and dancing as the room swirled around them. He closed his eyes tightly and then opened them again, cautiously, but now he could see nothing but bright white lights, as if something was pressing against his eyes. And then the pain came. He recognized it immediately, a livid, sharp stab across his chest. He tried to move his lips, but he felt like he was drowning, and if he opened his mouth, a huge wave would pour down his throat.

"He's burning up!" Grace exclaimed. "I'm sure he's having another attack. We have to get him to the hospital as soon as possible."

"All right," Seth called over his shoulder as he moved quickly out of the room. "I'll call an ambulance. You just stay with him."

Seth rushed into the living room. He picked up the land line phone and punched in the emergency number.

"Is he OK?" Lee asked, coming to stand beside him.

"It's an attack. I'm pretty sure of that. He's very sick."

"Will he make it?" Nick said, joining them.

"Only God knows that. But we can pray."

Seth spoke quickly into the phone, explained the situation, and gave the address. When he put the phone down, he could see that the others had gathered in the room, looking at him curiously, as if he had some secret information he could reveal to them.

"We just have to wait," he told them. "I have no idea.

Mom can stay with him."

The ambulance arrived almost immediately, and the orderlies carried Richard on a collapsible gurney out the side door. Grace accompanied them as they sped off to the hospital.

Standing in the living room, they could hear the siren fading and then nothing more except the distant thunder of the storm that had passed over the house. For a long while it seemed that no one wished to speak, as if something had changed the atmosphere in the room, and with it their purpose in being together had disappeared. Finally Deck spoke. Although he was standing next to Susan, he appeared not to notice that she was crying.

"It was that damned fishing trip. I have no doubt. And what he told us. Altogether too much of an effort for him. It's almost like he killed himself. He was so stubborn. If I believed in God, which I certainly don't, I'd say he was struck down for what he did."

"Is he going to die then?" Susan asked faintly. "I thought..."

"No, he's not," Seth said firmly. "And how could you say something terrible like that, Deck?"

"After what he did? Yes, I guess I'm entitled to say anything I want to. You agree with me, don't you, Nick? And he just invited us down here so he could make a scene in his final drama. What a bastard!"

Nick just stared ahead, trying to avoid looking at anyone. He was afraid that this awful moment would uncover old wounds and arouse forgotten animosities and jealousies among his brothers. Memories of the hurts they had inflicted on each other growing up would intensify any sharp things they said to each other now, whether they meant to injure or not. He just didn't have the energy to respond. Deck could be such a rat, he thought. And Seth. How could he not be hurt by what his father had just told them?

"You don't mean that, Deck. You don't," he said finally.

"No. Of course I don't. I wouldn't wish...."

There was a silence of futility again in the room. They all sensed it: the anger and the momentary relief. Finally Lee said:

"We were making lunch for you all, for when you got back. It's ready and the table is set. Maybe we should eat?"

Her suggestion seemed to revive everyone.

"I don't think I can eat anything," Susan said, reaching out to grab Deck's hand. "It's so sad!"

"No, I think it's a good idea," he said, brushing off her fingers and heading toward the dining room. "What else have we got to do while we wait?"

The rest of the group followed him, except for Susan who remained alone in the living room trying to compose herself. She finally joined them.

"Do we sit at our usual places?" Nick asked as he settled onto his chair.

"Without Mom and Dad, sure, why not?" Deck replied. "Except that I think I'll take his place for now. Since I'm the eldest."

"What?" said Nick, "You're not. Seth..."

"Oh, come on now, Nick," Deck said. "You know what I mean."

Seth thought that was uncalled for, an imposition, as if, suddenly, his younger brother decided to become the master of the family, but he said nothing. He saw no reason to call out what he thought was precipitous, unthinking behavior. Acting as if his father was already dead. But he let it pass.

Looking at Lee, sitting next to him, he took her hand in his, bowed his head, reaching across the table to Nick, and said:

"Lord, bless the food that we are about to eat and bless and nurture us and protect our father who is so gravely ill. Amen."

There was silence from the others who looked away in embarrassment. It was almost amusing, Seth thought when he noticed it, that a prayer could make some people so uncomfortable, and yet provide such hope and solace to others. He said nothing more and just took some of the lunch meats and salad from the platters that were passed around, and remained quiet.

For several more solemn minutes, no one said a word, as if eating required their absolute concentration. But finally, Seth cleared his throat and said:

"There's something I'd like to say about Dad. A funny story about a trip we took once. Before you were born, Nick, so of course you won't remember it, but Deck, you were there, sitting next to me in the back seat. I'm sure that we still had that old, blue Oldsmobile with the scraped right fender that Dad refused to get fixed, and it must have been about 1970—when I was eight. Dad and Mom were sitting in the front seat, and I remember we had gone about 100 miles down from Chicago, heading toward Southern Illinois to visit the relatives. It had to be a summer day—middle of July probably—because that's when Dad took his vacation every year. Mom was sitting with the map on her lap because there was a detour off the main road about two miles right outside of Decatur, and we were driving through corn fields..."

"For God's sake, Seth," Deck blurted out. "Shut up! No one wants to hear one of your shaggy dog stories now. And how could you remember so many things precisely? At that age? I don't believe you at all. Just fucking with us like you always do."

"I recall it quite clearly," Seth said, vaguely conscious of how much Deck had begun to sound just like his father.

"Yes, I guess you've always had a photographic memory for bullshit," Deck continued. "But I don't believe you for a moment. All that detail that adds up to absolutely zero. And now? Really? You always..."

Seth had stopped talking abruptly and looked at Lee, hoping that she would understand his silence. If Deck didn't want to hear something that might cheer them all up, that was his problem. And he wouldn't insist, even if it was a funny story. He realized that his brother was trying to assert something—his dominance? Did he think he had been reborn as the head of the family? Well, Seth would let him play at that; it certainly didn't matter to him. Or maybe that was the way he handled grief. For some people, he thought, anger might be comforting.

Susan stood up and, without looking at anyone, headed out of the dining room toward the kitchen. At the doorway, she turned back:

"I'll just put away the food and start on the dishes," she said, hoping that no one could see how embarrassed she was to listen to the brothers arguing.

It wasn't that she hadn't witnessed family squabbles before. Her mother and father frequently disagreed, and she couldn't count the number of times when their discussions disintegrated into long, bitter silences. But she wanted no part in someone else's family quarrels, and she told herself if she listened any more she was sure to find out something ugly about Deck, something that would make her regret this trip and what it had begun to reveal about him. And that would spoil everything. It *was* spoiling everything.

Lee left next, offering to help clear the table, and then, one by one, the brothers disappeared.

Eventually, in a roundabout way, Nick and Deck ended up together outside on the deck behind the house. The rain had stopped, leaving behind a slippery coating of water that pooled on the wooden planks. Both of them stood at the far edge, by the railing, looking out at the lake and the low clouds that raced across the sky trying to catch up to the storm.

"I can't feel any wind yet," Nick said, "but look at how fast everything seems to be moving."

Deck gave him a curious look: "It was a fucking mistake to go fishing. He wasn't up to it, that's for sure," he said. He felt in no mood to talk about the weather with his brother.

"But what a bastard!" he continued. "I didn't want to say much to him then—didn't want to give him the satisfaction. But I think I could have shoved him in the water. Drown him like a feral cat. What is he thinking, cutting us off like that?"

"Well, we'll get something, won't we?" Nick said after a minute.

"That's not the point. It's what it means. Oh, I'm sure he'll say that he wants all of us to make our way on our own, to prove ourselves. Same old story about rags to riches to justify himself, about how he made a go of it after a difficult childhood. He's said as much many times. And he probably thinks he's doing us a favor, but that's all screwed up and twisted. And anyway, does he really think we need a shove at this late date? We are who we are, aren't we already, Nick? You're certainly sure not going to change." He gave his brother a curious look.

"You don't need the money, do you, Deck? So why are you so upset?" Nick asked.

Deck looked at his brother but said nothing

"You don't, do you?" Nick asked.

"Well, I wasn't going to tell you, and you mustn't say a word to anyone."

"But?"

"But, I was going to ask Dad for a loan. Obviously now I won't get a chance. It's not that I'm broke or anything; far from it. But I wanted to set up my own business, break away from the firm. It's a great opportunity and I have everything lined up. But the deal is fragile. And what can I do now?"

"Can't you borrow from some bank?"

"You don't understand much, Nick. What do you know about business? No. Damn it! No!"

"I'm sorry, Deck."

"You should be. I mean, look at you. Crap job in a crap college. Don't you want to get out? Maybe go to New York or Europe somewhere. Paris? You've always wanted that. Start over."

"I'm doing OK," Nick said.

"But it's the principle of the thing, isn't it? He owes it to us and not to some law school and some students he'll never know about. I'm his God damned son after all! Sometimes I think you're pathetic."

"How do you think Seth feels?" Nick asked. "I think I'd be really hurt if I got an unequal share. Maybe we should give up part of ours to him, to make things equal."

"Are you completely nuts, Nick? Do you think he deserves the same as us? I mean, he's not really our brother after all. I'd say he's lucky to get anything. After all the fights and arguments he's had with Dad? But now that I think about it, I'll bet that his getting a smaller share compared to us would help us with the lawsuit."

Nick looked quizzically at his brother: "What lawsuit? What are you talking about?"

"I'm going to contest the will, of course. I'll drag his reluctant ghost into the courtroom. You can't cut off your immediate relatives like that. It can't be legal!"

"But he didn't. We all got something, even if it's pretty small."

"But maybe I'm going to break that will, and you and Seth—yes, even Seth—are going to help me do it."

"I don't know, Deck. Why can't we just leave it? I'd feel terrible."

"Because I don't want to give him the satisfaction," Deck continued, his voice rising.

"But he won't know, will he... when he's dead?"

"Except I'm going march right in and tell him as soon as he's conscious again, and you're going to be right there standing by my side, and even if you don't say one word, you can just nod your head in agreement, and he'll know what a losing situation he's created."

"I don't know. I'm not sure I want to get involved," Nick said, absently brushing away some of the water that had collected on the railing.

"You will, brother, you will, because you know it's

unfair. We're getting screwed."

"Are you sure that Seth will agree with this? I know he and Dad didn't get along very well, but sometimes he can be pretty stubborn."

"You let me deal with him. Maybe I'll suggest that he can give away everything to that fanatical church he belongs to now. In any case...."

Nick turned away from his brother, and then moved slowly back toward the house. But then he stopped and turned around.

"Do you really believe there's a chance we could actually break the will? I mean in court and everything? Don't you think he knows what's legal and not? He's always been so careful."

"Sure he knows. And the courts would obviously toss a case like that out. But I want everyone to know what a cruel and crazy old man he is—cutting off his sons. And I'm going to shove it in his face just for the pleasure of seeing him squirm."

"I don't know, Deck. It seems really mean when he's so sick. Do you really intend to go through with it?"

"Yeah. Just watch me!"

"Well, I guess it's OK to go back in," Nick said, turning away. "Lucky that Mom's not here right now. She'd certainly try to argue you out of it."

"Yeah, well, I've made up my mind. And maybe she wouldn't be so upset. After all, the will sets up that living trust, but without trusting her. I don't know who he's appointed as executor. We didn't get that far, did we? But I'll bet it's some god-damned lawyer crony of his, like he couldn't rely on any of us."

Nick looked at his brother as if he could see something

in him he had never quite known before. He understood that Deck had been deeply hurt by their father's tight-fisted scheme. He was too, if he admitted it. But he wasn't sure he would agree to help in any lawsuit. True enough, a larger inheritance would make his own life much easier. He might be able to give up the routine of private lessons. If he really wanted to. And maybe he could get a big enough place so that Mark could move in. Maybe even buy a house and get a dog like they had always talked about. Or they could travel. But, as he thought about it, the person really offended ought to be Seth. Sure, he was adopted, but he wondered if that was a good reason to single him out like that. He just didn't understand his father. There had been too many revelations during this trip already, and he almost feared what might come next. He decided he should call Mark sometime soon and ask him what he thought. And Deck would have to face his father alone. He just wasn't up to that. He wouldn't agree no matter what his brother said.

Seth was sitting slouched in an armchair in the living room, his eyes closed. When Nick entered, he sat up abruptly, as if he had been roused from sleep.

"Didn't mean to disturb you, Seth," Nick said.

"I was just thinking. Worrying, I guess. I'd really like to know what's going on at the hospital. I've half decided to go myself."

"Won't Mom be home soon?"

"You never know, I guess so. But, I think someone ought to be with her."

Nick waited a moment before saying anything more.

He wanted to approach what he had in mind exactly the right way, and he knew he wasn't very good at saying anything difficult. It was always a problem talking to Seth because, in his own mind, he could only think of the differences between them. They had never been close, and now, Nick could only imagine what his brother thought of him. He had never said a word about his having a boyfriend, but, of course, everyone seemed to know or at least sense it. And he wondered if Seth's religion would condemn him—if Seth would judge him for being who he was. And he might interpret what he was about to say as somehow connected to that.

"There's something I need to tell you," he began cautiously, "that I want to say."

He sat down on the sofa across from Seth, but leaned forward so he could be closer.

"I'm really sorry about what Dad told us he's planning to do. There's no call for it, and I think you're getting screwed, and I think the reason for that really sucks."

Seth just looked at him and said nothing, so he continued:

"I know that as brothers we haven't always been close, and now more than ever we've gone our own ways. But I wanted to tell you what Deck intends to do. To warn you. And let you know before he springs it on you, so you can think about it."

Seth continued to stare at him, and Nick was feeling more and more uncomfortable. Why, he wondered, had he taken it on himself to be the messenger boy when he was sure Deck would inform his brother soon enough? But he had started, and there was no way to cut this short.

"Deck's planning to contest the will in court, or at

least tell Dad that's what he intends to do, and he wants both of us to join in a lawsuit. Try to break the will. And he especially wants you to be part of it, because...."

Seth took a long time to respond, and what he said was certainly not anything Nick expected:

"I think I'll drive over to the hospital now to see how Dad's doing. Waiting around for a phone call can be pretty terrible. And Mom needs our support. You can come with me if you want."

"But what do you think?"

"What? About Deck? Some lawsuit?"

"Yes."

"Well, I guess I'm not surprised."

He stood up and started to leave the room.

"The answer is 'no' Nick," he said, turning back. "I'm surprised you even mentioned it. And now I'm going to tell Lee I'm leaving, and if you want to come along, just meet me outside by the camper."

"OK," Nick said, "But why don't we take their car? I'll find the keys and you can drive if you want. And you should think about what I said and listen to Deck."

"No, Nick. I won't. But glad you're coming along."

"Should I tell Deck?"

"Anything you want, sure."

Seth disappeared, leaving Nick alone. He glanced toward the door that opened onto the outside, but then followed his brother out of the living room to search for the keys to his parents' car. It made him feel terrible to be stretched between his two siblings. Deck had always accused him of being weak and indecisive, and maybe that was true. But this was becoming an impossible situation, and he wasn't sure which would end worse: the serious condition of his father or the knowledge that there was certain to be a bitter confrontation over the will. He wanted no part of that.

CHAPTER 10

Grace was sitting on a flimsy plastic chair in a small alcove off the hallway that led to an operating theater and several examining rooms further on. She didn't know where they had taken Richard, and she looked up anxiously whenever anyone in scrubs passed by. She had been tempted to call out and demand to know where he was, but something made her hesitate. She would know soon enough; they would have to tell her when they knew something, and maybe she didn't want to know. She just had to be here, to wait.

She stared down at the gleaming linoleum floor, and for some odd reason the image of a night workman walking slowly behind a slithering polishing machine moving slowly from one side of the corridor to the other, came to mind. That's how they must get these floors so clean, she thought. There was no reason to imagine this except that she knew in this moment of anxious boredom that she was trying to think of anything but the present and the instant when some door would open suddenly, and the doctor—their GP, Dr. Travis—would appear to pronounce sentence on her husband. Her mind was racing, and every possibility she considered was dreadful in its own way. Whatever the news, it would be terrible, only different. If he had died, then she would be flung into an awful enveloping grief. She had no idea how she could face that. That was something unknown and foreign to her, and she had, until recently, refused to imagine it. Of course she had lamented the passing of her mother and father, but that had been years ago, and she had forgotten the feelings of their loss.

But if the doctor said he would live, and could come home again, then the uncertainty of waiting would begin again. She wasn't sure she could cope with that any longer. Once the boys left, he would surely need a professional nurse, perhaps full time, and someone who would move into one of the bedrooms would become a constant interference. She was afraid she couldn't bear that.

She moved slightly in the uncomfortable chair on its spindly metal legs, and then eased herself forward to peer down the hallway again to see if she could glimpse some activity. But she could see nothing except the bright lights reflecting on the pale blue walls. She sat back again, wondering why they had chosen that color. Of course red would have been entirely inappropriate, and she almost laughed at the thought—and the obvious metaphor. But the color scheme was blue everywhere: the plastic chair, the walls, even the accent pattern on the floor and the color of the scrubs the doctor wore. She had noticed that the orderlies and nurses wore a deeper shade to differentiate them in a color scheme that she imagined reinforced the hierarchy of the staff.

If she stayed long enough, sitting upright in this stiff, inadequate chair, she feared she would begin to imagine more than she ever wanted to know about this place, in order not to think.

But why was there no news yet, she wondered; why was it taking them so long?

She glanced at the tiny gold watch on her left wrist. She could barely make out the time, and it reminded her that she ought to buy something more visible now, with larger numbers and distinct hands. Her eyes certainly weren't what they once were. But it had been her mother's, and she was reluctant to take it off. There was so little to remember her by.

She thought she'd already been waiting almost an hour; it seemed so in hospital time, at least. Surely they knew something by now. For a moment, she wondered if they were keeping the bad news from her.

But, she corrected herself. Doctors didn't blanch at telling you something you didn't want to hear. She was aware of that. She looked at her watch again.

If she only had something to read. But she knew she would be unable to concentrate. Better just to close her eyes and drift among her memories, trying to sort through them to find something pleasant, something from her childhood.

Shutting out the glare of the harsh illumination was a relief, and she felt almost light-headed, as if she had been released from some vague but persistent discomfort.

She heard a voice, drifting from somewhere in the distance, calling to her. She knew she shouldn't be peeking into her mother's jewelry box, but something moved her hand and she pulled out a paste necklace and held it up to her neck in front of the mirror on the dressing table. She tried to put it back quickly, but it didn't seem to fit anywhere. The voice became more insistent, and she fumbled with the lid of the box, which wouldn't close.

"Mrs. Collins," the voice called again.

She woke suddenly and saw Dr. Travis standing in front of her.

"Oh, I'm so sorry," she said. "I must have fallen asleep for a moment. Please tell me, how is he?"

"About as well as can be expected," he said. "It was a false alarm. I don't know what brought it on. You know patients with a serious condition like his can imagine all sorts of things—even excruciating pain. We're pretty sure that this episode—whatever it was—has been caused by something emotional perhaps—it certainly wasn't another heart attack, although he seems weaker than the last time I saw him. Has he been under undue stress today? That can sometimes mimic a cardiac incident."

"Well, he was out in the boat on the lake with his sons. And then that storm came up. He was very wet by the time they brought him in."

"Now, Mrs. Collins, Grace, I have to insist that such strenuous activity can be very dangerous. I thought you would know better. I realize that he's a very stubborn man, but anything physical like that is completely out of the question. He needs rest. Constant rest. And you need to make sure that he doesn't get upset. That can be just as serious."

"I know that, Doctor. But he's a difficult man."

"I'm going to keep him here overnight, just as a precaution, and I'll release him tomorrow morning. You can pick him up around ten o'clock. Do you have someone to help you? I think he's going to need more assistance from now on, and it may be beyond you."

He looked at her as if he was gauging her strength.

"I doubt if you will be able to manage by yourself," he continued. "He's not a small man. So I suggest that you either hire a nurse or some full-time helper, or perhaps we can arrange for him to be placed in assisted living. That might be best for everyone."

"No!" she said firmly. "No. He'd never agree to that."

"Perhaps he'll have no choice. Can you make him understand that? I could talk to him, of course. Maybe coming from me it...."

"No, Doctor. I'll try to think of something. Maybe one of his sons can stay on for awhile."

"If you think so, but it could be several months... or tomorrow. I can't predict how long it will be."

Grace blinked away the tears that had suddenly blurred her vision. She leaned over to pick up her purse that was set up against her chair, thinking that she might find a handkerchief. And then she set it down again and looked up.

"I'll see what we can do," she said. "He can be so cantankerous."

"I suppose that's a good sign, Mrs. Collins. At least he hasn't given up yet. But I think you understand that it could be any moment now. You need to prepare yourself."

"Yes," she said. "I know, and I'll do my best. I'll make do."

He looked at her curiously for a moment and then said: "Fine. Good."

"And can I see him now?"

"You can look in if you want, but he's asleep. We've given him a sedative. We moved him to room 207. Just continue down the corridor and then turn left. You'll find it. Or ask one of the nurses. But please don't try to wake him."

He smiled briefly, bent over and touched her hand,

and then walked back in the opposite direction.

She watched him until he disappeared, and then she stood up, clutched her purse, and started to walk slowly, almost unwillingly, toward her husband's room. She knew she should be relieved that he was still alive, but seeing him, no matter how peacefully sleeping, would just remind her of how difficult the coming days were going to be. She knew she ought to feel a respite, but she couldn't. Did she want him to die? Was that awful idea what distressed her and twisted her thoughts into a tangle of guilt and depression? Why else was she so hesitant to see him? She was already exhausted.

Standing in front of the door to the ward where he had been removed, she peeked through the small window to see if she could spot him. There were two beds, both occupied, but it was impossible to identify either of the patients. She opened the door cautiously and entered. His bed was nearest the window, and a pale light from it fell on the stark white sheets and blanket that shrouded him. Only his face and bare arms emerged from the covering. As she approached, she could see that his eyes were shut and the skin of his cheeks was flushed. He had an oxygen tube attached to his nose and a drip in his arm. A monitor by the side of the bed beeped faintly. His chest rose and fell almost imperceptibly.

If she spoke to him, if she told him her thoughts, if she let him know all her doubts and worries, maybe he would hear even if he couldn't respond. There were so many things she wanted to say to him. She had tried to change his mind about the will and failed. It was truly awful what he had done to his sons, and especially to Seth. She wondered if, somehow, when he told them, sitting in the boat in the middle of the lake with the storm bearing down on them—he had felt guilty, and his remorse had brought on this attack, or whatever it was. But she didn't really believe in that kind of natural reckoning. Nonetheless, she thought it—the possibility of it. Who wouldn't imagine, if only for a minute, that Nature or God or whatever mysterious force had exacted justice just at that moment? But only Seth, with his fervent belief, might ever seriously suggest that. And she doubted that he would say a word even if he believed it.

There was a chair set beside his bed, and she sat down, dropping her purse on the floor beside her. She reached out and took his hand, and he stirred slightly but didn't awaken. She just stared at his face. She tried to imagine the young, energetic man she had married fifty years before, and the long hours when they had planned their life together. But she had come to realize something she had never allowed herself to think until now. During those early moments of hope and speculation, it was always his life that they seemed to be discussing. She hadn't listened carefully, perhaps because she was in the thrall of love—and she hadn't paid attention or hadn't recognized then that his ambition and love of the law were always going to be an impediment between them. She had been so young and naïve, and now, when she finally did understand, she had to accept that the body of law was the body that he had always cherished most.

She looked up when she heard the door open and saw that Nick and Seth had just entered.

"How is he, Mom?" Seth asked, walking quickly to her side and placing his hand on her shoulder.

She stood up and hugged him: "It wasn't a heart attack, the Doctor said. Thank goodness for that! Maybe something emotional. Like a panic attack."

"That's a relief. But how are you? You look awfully pale," Seth said.

"I'm just tired. Exhausted from everything that's happened today, and the constant worry."

"Nick and I will take you home if you're ready to leave."

Seth approached the bed, closed his eyes, bowed his head, and mumbled something inaudible while Nick just stood at the foot of the bed.

"Just a minute more," she said, looking down at Richard. She was trying to feel sympathy; she didn't think she should leave before she felt sympathy. Maybe she should pray too? Like Seth? But for what, she wondered?

"When will they release him?" Seth asked, touching his father's shoulder briefly and then turning toward her.

"Tomorrow at ten. They gave him a sedative and he'll probably sleep all night."

She looked away and turned to walk toward the door, almost stumbling. Seth grabbed her arm to steady her.

"All right," she said, "I'm ready. Let's go."

"Nick? Are you coming?"

"Yes," he said, staring down at his father. "He looks so still. Did you notice? Are you sure he's OK? I can hardly see him breathing."

"Doctor Travis was certain," Grace said. "They gave him all sorts of tests. But he's very weak of course."

Nick seemed reluctant to leave and edged closer to his father's body. He reached down and touched his arm. He said nothing and then looked away abruptly and started to move toward the door to join his mother and Seth.

CHAPTER 11

Back at the lake the three brothers met in the living room. Light from a single, weak lamp just seemed to accent the gloom of the late afternoon. Deck and Nick both had poured themselves a drink and sat glumly looking at each other, waiting for the moment to begin their inevitable discussion with Seth.

Susan, Lee and Grace had announced they were going for a walk, despite the wet ground left over from the storm. Grace, who suggested it, realized that the brothers wanted to be alone, and she feared that there might be angry voices. She had been stricken with more than enough intense emotion for one day—for a lifetime, she had thought, all compacted into a few hours.

Walking outside, Susan clutched Grace's arm as the three women made their way carefully down the steps of the slippery deck toward the dock where the boat was tied up.

"There's a path around the lake just over there," Grace explained as she pointed the way. "We can always turn back if it's too muddy.

As they walked on, the trees released brief showers

when the wind shook their branches. But the path was relatively dry.

"It's the one thing I love about living here," Grace said, "the woods, the wildlife and the lake. It seems to create its own weather—so changeable."

"Don't you miss Chicago?" Susan asked.

"Yes, of course I do. But Richard insisted on coming here and I agreed."

When Susan said nothing, Grace continued: "You know, you get into the habit of saying yes. Someone has to."

They walked on in silence across an open field, past several houses, and then followed the trail as it turned into a patch of damp woods.

"You live in the country, don't you, Lee... you and Seth?" Grace said, slowing down for a moment.

"Yes, Mother, but it's nothing like this. It's always bright where we are, and always summer. But here reminds me of my home place."

"Don't you miss it?" Susan asked, catching up to Lee.

"No," Lee said. "I want to be here. There is nothing for me where I came from. Only sad memories."

They continued on, silent again, following the path where it turned down almost to the lake, when suddenly they encountered a large pool of water.

"I suppose we should turn back now," Grace said, stopping. And then she looked carefully at her two companions, reaching out to touch them.

"You are both so lovely," she exclaimed. "I wish... it would be so nice to have you stay."

And then she turned away.

"I'm sorry. I know that's impossible. Sometimes I think

I must be strange. I wonder about myself. But now I suppose we ought to turn back," she said, stiffening. "I'm sure the men folks are waiting for us."

As they sat together in the living room, Seth looked at his brothers and laughed:

"You both look awful. Dad's going to be OK, at least for a while. It was a false alarm, and you ought to be happy about it."

Deck looked up at him, setting down his drink on the rug next to his chair.

"It's not that, Seth. All good and well that he didn't die this time, but it can't be much longer."

"Maybe. But there's always hope, isn't there? So what's bothering you two, then, to be so gloomy all of a sudden?"

"I don't know what right you have to be so happy; it's like you don't care," Nick blurted out.

"But I really do," Seth said quickly. "I'm awfully pleased that Dad is going to be coming home tomorrow. You know that."

"That's not what he means," Deck said, seeming to realize that he had to take charge of the conversation. He feared that Nick would just meander around: he was too disorganized and timid to say anything outright. He'd just wobble intolerably, like a table with a short leg, he thought. So it was up to him.

"For God's sake, wake up, Seth!" he almost shouted: "What Nick is referring to is that fucking will. Dad's will. What a bastard! You can't tell me you're not disappointed. All three of us should be—and you especially—for the way he screwed you."

Seth just looked at him and said nothing. If he shook his head, Deck didn't notice.

"Aren't you upset? I mean, what a nasty thing to do to you!"

"It's his money," Seth said. "And as long as Mom is provided for, I don't care. Not for myself, at least."

"But he fucked us all. Leaving almost everything to the University law school and bribing them to name it after him. Yeah, that's what I'd call it—giving them our inheritance so they'll put his name on a building. What kind of man does that to his sons? It's a rotten thing."

Seth just shrugged his shoulders.

"I guess he has his reasons for everything," he said.

"Well, don't you want to do something about it?" Deck asked. "I can't understand you. You just sit there and justify something really mean-spirited. I know you could use the money; certainly more than either of us. I'm sure that little business of yours, whatever the hell it is, can barely keep you and your wife alive. Come on, Seth. Grow up! You need to stand up for yourself!"

"Lee and I do OK," Seth said. "We've got enough."

"But think of what you could do for your church," Nick said.

"Shut up, Nick!" Deck said, glaring at him. "Let me do the talking. You'll just screw everything up!"

Nick shrank down in his chair, looked around for his drink, and then took a large gulp. The sharpness of the liquor made him wince, and the warmth of the alcohol made him shiver. He decided that he would keep quiet and let Deck talk. It was his plan, after all; whatever it was going to be.

"So here's what I want to do," Deck said. "And I want

you; we both want you, Seth, Nick and I, both want you to join in with us. All the brothers acting together."

He hesitated and then continued, "I'm going to... we are going to contest the will in court. Give the old man back as good as he deserves. And as soon as he comes home and is alert enough to understand what's happening, I'm going to tell him. I don't care how sick he is. That's why we need you, Seth, especially you, to stand with us, because you're the one person most hurt by his tightfistedness."

He stopped for a minute. "No," he continued, "I mean his cruelty; let me be frank: that's the only word for it. Almost cutting you off entirely and just throwing Nick and me a couple of bare bones!"

Seth started to stand up and then dropped back down onto the sofa where he had been sitting:

"I don't think so, Deck," he said, finally. "If Dad wants to do whatever with his money, I don't care. Not at all. So, the answer is no. I'm not going to be a part of some lawsuit against my own family. How could you even imagine that?"

"But Seth," Nick said. "It's not even your..."

He was going to continue, but Deck looked at him sternly, and he stopped. He wasn't sure what he was going to say to Seth, but he wasn't sure he wanted to be a part of some lawsuit against his father's will, even if it was only a threat. But Deck seemed so determined to go on, and he had always gone along with his older brother—at least to appear if he would. But he really didn't know what to do.

"Seth, listen to me for once in your life and don't speak until I've finished," Deck said. "Maybe we haven't always gotten along very well, and sometimes, I admit, I haven't treated you the way you deserved—as the brother you are—but this is an emergency. It's a time for us to stick together and stand up to him—Dad."

Seth said nothing, and Nick watched him, fascinated to hear what he was going to say. For years, he had resented Seth—no, that wasn't the right word for it. He had just disliked him for being a constant irritant in the family, for all the arguments with his father, and the sullen dinners where Seth told his stories and infuriated his father. His always demanding attention and then squandering it. He was different, just different, and they had never been anything more than brothers in name. Maybe he, Nick, hadn't tried hard enough to understand. Maybe none of them had really tried. And now, this was the result. He didn't know what was going to happen.

"You need to consider this carefully, Seth," Deck said. "And if we go on without you and try to break the will, and you're not included, well, you won't get a penny out of it."

"Is that fair?" Nick said.

"You're damned right it's fair," Deck said, cutting him off. "If he's too cowardly to join in and fight for what we're owed, then why should he get anything? Think about it, Seth."

Seth stood up and began to walk slowly toward the dining room.

"I think I'll get a glass of water. Either of you want anything?" he said. "And I'm sorry, Deck, for both of you, actually, but I'm not going to be a part of your plan, whatever it is. Have you even thought of Mom at all? How do you think she would react to such a threat?"

"She'll get her share," Deck said. "So why should she worry?"

"That's certainly not the point, is it?" Seth said.

When he was almost out of the room, Deck called after him:

"You never were part of this family, damn you, Seth! And now you're just making things worse!"

Seth just looked back at him and continued out of the room.

"You didn't need to say that," Nick said. "You don't really think that helped, do you?"

"Fuck you, Nick," Deck said, softly. "Fuck you and your vacillation. No wonder you're a...."

He stopped without finishing his sentence, and then resumed:

"Don't you realize that a united front is the only way we could ever make a statement, and if Seth won't join us, I don't think there's much of a chance now. You're almost on his side, aren't you? I can see it in your guilty face."

"Come on, Deck. Cut it out," Nick said. "And who I am and how I lead my life is my own business. So cut out the remarks! But maybe I'll try to talk to him later. You sure don't help things by tossing angry words around like that. That never helped much with him. But I'm pretty sure he won't change his mind. And for what it's worth, I think it's a terrible idea. You're not concerned for all of us—just yourself; why don't you admit it?"

After saying this, Nick looked away, because he didn't want to see what effect his sudden harsh—brave—words would have.

Deck just scowled and headed out onto the deck, leaving his brother alone.

*

Nick watched his brother go and then left the living room and ducked into his bedroom to call Mark. Sitting on the bed, with his cellphone in hand, he punched in the number, although he had no idea what he wanted to say. Perhaps it was just the idea of escaping for a moment from the sadness and anger that engulfed them all here: he wanted a lifeline—like a buoy tossed out to someone drowning in tension.

"Hi Mark," he said, "it's Nick."

"I've rather expected you would call at some point. How's it going? How is your Dad?"

"It's worse than I thought," he said. And then he paused.

"Are you there still there, Nick?"

"Yes. I just don't know what to say. I only wanted to hear a friendly voice."

"I'm a lot more than that," Mark said.

"Yes, I know. Of course. I'm sorry. It's just that everything gets turned upside down when I'm back here—back to being the youngest son and watching them all tear each other apart."

"Is it that bad? Did both your brothers show up?"

"Yes, to my regret."

"From what you've told me..."

"Yeah, but I don't want to talk about them now."

"OK. Sorry. Didn't mean anything."

"It's OK. Really. I'm just unhappy. It brings back too many memories."

"When are you coming home?"

"Soon, Mark. And thank you for saying that."

"What? What did I say?"

"Home. That's what I mean. Where I belong. Not here. Home with you."

"I'm glad you said that too, Nick. Hurry back."

"All right. Goodbye."

"Yes."

Nick tossed the cellphone by his side and stretched out on the bed. He wasn't sure why he felt better, but he did, and it was comforting just to be away from the rest of them, if only until he was sure they missed him.

Later that evening, they all gathered at the dining room table for a cold meal, their silences punctuated only by an occasional remark or question that no one seemed to want to answer.

Grace had spent a long time alone in the kitchen, just sitting, with a cup of cold tea in front of her. Whenever Lee or Susan dared enter, offering to help make dinner, she shooed them out, demanding to be left alone. She thought if she kept to herself, without having to deal with their sympathy, she could just about manage to carry on. Of course she wondered exactly what Richard had told his sons about the will, and how they had reacted, although, from the anguished way Deck and Nick kept looking at each other, she feared the worst. It occurred to her that Richard's panic attack must have started on the boat just after he revealed his intentions. The thought occurred to her again—silly and completely preposterous—that the moment was like some Shakespearean tragedy where the heavens announced the dark happenings of the play with thunder and lightning. Like that wonderful production of *Macbeth* she and Richard had seen when that traveling English company had come to Chicago: when they were still courting. When the witches were chanting. She remembered it distinctly now. So long ago, when they were courting and everything was the future.

Goodness, she thought, that had been ages since—three sons ago, and a thousand lonely nights when he was sitting in the living room with his beloved yellow pads writing out his briefs, and she, just like tonight, would be sitting alone in the kitchen with a cup of cold tea as her companion. She wondered if the worry of this moment and the bother of a house full of anxiety was somehow forcing her to remember only the disappointments of her life with him. Surely they had shared many moments of happiness, and she had always loved him deeply, almost in spite of herself. But their periods of joy and intimacy had almost always happened when he was away from the law, and on vacation somewhere. and not immersed in some case. "Damn the law, damn that demanding mistress of his!" she whispered.

When they were first married, he seemed happy to travel—once they went abroad to France and Italy, where she was utterly charmed by his attention and companionship. But as the years had accumulated and the boys were growing up, their lives became a ritual of lonely days and nights for her, and he seemed more and more in the thrall of legal matters, continually shutting her out.

Early in their marriage, she had thought to get a job, even if only volunteer work. There was so much that she wanted to do. But on every occasion she suggested it, he had seemed offended and hurt, and she couldn't bear that. And, of course, there had always been the boys to look after. Perhaps if she had been stronger, if she had insisted at the beginning, she would not feel so desperate now—if she had created her own life and a history separate from his. But now it seemed as if she had been absorbed into him, and when he was gone, she could only retrieve half of her existence.

Finally, she had roused herself to make dinner. Long before anyone had arrived, she had bought all the ingredients for a chicken casserole—a dish that had been the boys' favorite. But tonight, when she finally managed to serve it, she realized that she had undercooked some of the vegetables and the sauce was thin and watery.

"I'm sorry," she said when she presented it. "I don't know what happened."

"I'm sure it's great," Lee said as the serving dish was passed to her. "God bless you Mother. We really appreciate you."

Grace didn't even have the energy to protest at that. Let her say anything she wants, she thought. What in the world did that matter now?

What she wanted to know, most of all, was exactly what Richard had told them and how they had reacted. Perhaps the silence, the glowering silence around the table, was answer enough. Her sons would be furious, and they had every right to be. Except not, it seemed, Seth, who had started to tell one of his stories—some memory that she had entirely forgotten—until Lee had put a firm hand on his, and he had stopped mid-sentence.

For some reason, looking at those two, she wondered what they had to be happy about. When Richard died, Seth would inherit only a tiny bequest—not enough to make any difference in their difficult lives. She wondered how they managed as it was. But he seemed unfazed by what Richard had told them, unlike Nick and Deck, especially Deck, who looked almost desperate, as if he had been visited by some dreadful portent. And poor Susan, dragged into the midst of a family drama that was both mourning and incensed at the same time. Why in the world had

Deck brought her here to witness this? How unthinking he was!

Grace could see that everyone was uncomfortable, wanting this meal to end, but something kept them all at the table, a few words uttered now and then, but no real conversation. And no one ate very much—except Seth. Finally, she realized it was up to her to break up this sullen gathering.

"I'll accept some help with the dishes," she said, suddenly standing up. "Any volunteers?"

Seth said, "Sure, Mom. We'd be glad to." He pushed his chair back and picked up his plate. "I'll carry these in. Why doesn't everyone else just sit in the living room? Lee and I can do everything. Maybe fix yourselves a drink. We can figure out where everything goes."

Without another word said, the plates were passed down to Seth, and then, one by one, the others left the room.

In the kitchen, Lee looked under the sink for a garbage can. "No one seemed to eat anything," she said. "I hate to waste all this food."

"I thought it was pretty good," Seth said, laughing, "despite half the ingredients missing. Yes, I'll bet she got a new recipe out of the Minimal Cookbook!"

"You're so silly, sometimes!" Lee said. "You always make a joke of things."

"Should I be upset then? Did you see the faces of my brothers? I couldn't be like them."

"Maybe you just don't care, Seth. Have you ever thought of that?"

"Oh, I care. I care a lot. But just not for the things that make them sad. I care for you and for our lives and for my garden... and my faith." He stopped and smiled at her. He started to hug her, but she held up her wet hands.

"Later!" she said.

In the living room, the two sons and Susan arranged themselves, perhaps unconsciously, in a semi-circle around Grace. Deck poured a stiff drink for everyone.

"I don't usually take such strong medicine," Grace said, trying to make a joke because she felt terribly uncomfortable with everyone watching her, waiting for her to say something.

"After your day, Mom," Nick said, "you're more than entitled."

She just nodded.

"You're all waiting for me to ask," she said finally. "So, all right, I will. Did he tell you?"

"Yes, out on the boat, just before the storm broke. Didn't give any real details, but yes, he said his worst." Deck looked at Susan as he said this, as if he wanted her not to listen. She blushed and turned away.

"I'm sorry for you, boys," Grace said. "And I wonder what Seth thought. It was so mean, especially to him."

"Who cares about Seth?" Deck said. "He lives in his own world. It's like he's untouchable. Anyway, why does it matter? He's adopted, isn't he? Not really one of us."

"That's a terrible thing to say," Grace said. "You can be so awful sometimes, Deck."

"I feel awful; you're damned right," he replied. "I've just been screwed out of a lot of money that I needed. No wonder I feel terrible. I have good reasons."

"I tried to talk him out of it, you know," Grace said. "We had some pretty tense moments."

"But he persisted, right? Is anyone surprised at that?

He always did get his way! You'd have to be the first person to admit that."

"Oh, Deck!"

"Don't be upset, Mom," Nick said. "I'm sure you tried your best."

"But we're not going to let it happen," Deck continued. "We're going to break that will. I mean, not really, but we're going to threaten to. He has no right, I'm sure, no moral right to treat his natural sons that way. Maybe, in the end, we'll go through with it and drag his memory into court. I don't know. In any case, that's what we're going to tell him, and he'll know that everyone will realize what a stingy bastard he is."

"You can't tell him that," Grace said, almost shouting. "Please, Deck. Whatever you're going to do—and I beg you not to do it—please don't say anything to him. Not now when he's so ill."

She put her hands up to her face to hide her expression and the tears that were beginning to stream down.

"Haven't I got enough worries," she sobbed, "without you boys...."

"Well, not all of us," Nick said. "Seth refuses to object to the will. And I really don't care."

"I guess he realizes he deserves what he doesn't get," Deck said.

"Son, please!" Grace sobbed. "Sometimes you go too far. Stop it. Seth's your brother."

"I'm sorry, Mom," Deck said. "But the reality is the reality. Seth never really belonged among us. I actually feel bad for him, and I don't mean to be cruel, but facts are facts."

"You sound like your father, sometimes, Deck—at his

worst," Grace said, wiping her eyes with a handkerchief that she pulled out of her pocket: "It's not just facts or what's legal. There's more in life than that."

"I'm proud to be like him," Deck said. "If it means facing life head-on and looking reality in the canines."

"And sometimes you too can really be a bastard," Nick added.

"Though in your interest, Baby Brother, though in your interest," Deck replied. "We're going to let everyone know about that will no matter what. Dad has no right. At least you're going to be OK, Mom. At least that."

"I don't care so much for myself," Grace said, trying to control her voice. "I just hate to see you boys so bitter. It's even worse than I thought. I warned him. But he's so stubborn. I think his being sick has made him more determined. But what you're planning to do is simply terrible. I can't agree to that. Please don't say anything. For my sake."

No one seemed to notice that Susan was still present, sitting anxiously on the edge of her chair, ready to bolt out of the room at any lull in the conversation that would allow her to excuse herself. She couldn't decide if she was just fascinated or horrified by all the frank and angry words. And she couldn't take her eyes off Deck. What he said about his father and his brother was appalling, she thought. But then, who was she to judge? She was just an outsider who was an unwilling witness to the unraveling of a family. But who was right? And did she have any reason to care?

She knew nothing of their history—not really—and if she thought about her own sisters and parents, she realized that no casual visitor, listening into a conversation among them, would ever be able to catch the nuances that trailed their years of experiences with each other. Or the reasons behind what they said—the half-sentences and allusions that only she would understand.

"I think I ought to leave," she said, finally standing because she sensed an interlude of quiet. "I'll see if I can help in the kitchen."

She tip-toed out of the room carefully as if she might step on some fragile object. She didn't look back. Deck glanced in her direction without really seeing her and said, calmly, at last:

"I'm sorry about all this, Mom. But I think that Dad is being terribly unfair. I know there's no chance for him to write a new will—not enough time for that. But I think everyone will see things our way."

"You'll do what you're going to do, I suppose," Grace said. "But now, I have a splitting headache and I'm going to go to bed. You'll say good night to the others for me, won't you? Make my excuses."

It had been a terrible, long day, she thought, although still early, but if emotions counted as minutes, then the hours had accumulated well beyond nightfall, and beyond what anyone should have to experience in so short a time.

"Good night, boys," she said, facing straight ahead as she reached the archway leading toward her bedroom. She didn't turn back to look at them because, at that moment, she couldn't bear to see their faces.

When Susan entered the kitchen, Seth and Lee were just putting away the last dishes. Lee was wearing an apron, and she wiped her hands on it and then untied the waist-bands. It hung loose from the loop around her neck.

"I was hoping to help a bit," Susan said. "But I see you've finished. I'm sorry. I should have..."

"No problem," Seth said. "We're just going to say good night and go out to the camper."

If she had the nerve, Susan thought she should warn them not to enter the living room. But who was she to run interference for the brother she didn't even know?

"Then I'll see you tomorrow morning," she said.

Seth watched her leave the kitchen and then said to Lee, who had removed the apron:

"I'll tell them good night—whoever's left in the living room. You go on outside; I'll be just a minute."

He didn't add that he fully expected his brothers, if they were still up, to be huddled together in a serious discussion rehearsing their plot. Somehow this situation reminded him of a story, maybe it was something from the Bible—but he wasn't sure which one. No, as he thought about it, he was pretty certain that there were no parables that could match the circumstances that he found himself in. Except, now it dawned on him, yes, it was actually like the whole of mankind's rebellion against God's judgment—this refusal to accept what was mysterious justice handed down by the Father. Yes, he thought, the will was just like that. He was glad he thought of it.

He walked into the living room and noticed that his brothers were quiet, looking glum and exhausted, but sitting far apart, as if the distance measured some disagreement.

"I'll say good night," he said, and started to leave.

"Just so you know," Nick said. "Deck is on his own if he wants to make trouble about the will. I just can't. Seeing Dad in the hospital and all. And Mom. I can't."

"So that's that," Seth said, looking at Deck.

"Yeah, brother. That's that."

The next morning, the passing storm delivered a day that was bright and crisp, with only a few white clouds hanging motionless in a luminous blue sky. Grace was up early because sleep had been impossible. She couldn't remember a night spent like that. It surprised her that what kept her awake weren't the events of the day, or even the worry about Richard and the bitterness caused by the revelation of his terrible will. Instead, when she closed her eyes, there were only uncomfortable memories: haunting recollections of the times she had snapped at friends or her children, or had done something she deeply regretted and couldn't undo. Why this? Why this rehearsal of moments when she felt such guilt? And everything was as vivid and inexorable as a nightmare. She didn't understand, except that it must be her unconscious fear that somehow she was at fault for failing to keep Richard from making his strange and unfair bequests.

Maybe, she considered, if she had put her disagreements differently or if she had been more forceful, she might have dissuaded him. Yes, and if she had asserted herself from the very beginning even, when they had first planned to marry, things might be different now. But how would that have been possible? She didn't want to admit that their relationship had always been at his convenience, but maybe it was, and now the family that she had so cautiously nurtured was being ripped apart. Was it her fault? Her weakness? Why should she blame herself that the law had always come first for him? How would that have mattered? It was a life she had chosen and a man she had loved.

The telephone began to ring, but she just stared at the receiver. She was afraid to answer. Of course, it might only be a robo-call; they seemed to start earlier and earlier recently. But she knew, of course, that it was the hospital or Dr. Travis on the other end. But whatever the news, if Richard had suddenly taken a turn for the worse... or if he was to be released to return home, she was frightened by either possibility. She didn't want to know how this continuing drama would end or when it would end.

Reluctantly, she picked up the receiver:

"Hello," she said quietly. "Grace Collins speaking."

"This is Dr. Travis," said the firm voice. "We have some good news. Your husband is well enough to come home this morning. I've arranged for his release. There are a few medications he'll need to take, which I'll send along, and he'll need lots of rest, of course. Bed rest and absolutely no stress."

She said nothing.

"Are you still on the line, Mrs. Collins, Grace?"

"Yes," she said finally. "That's wonderful news. Can I send one of the boys over to pick him up?"

"No," he said. "I'd prefer him to come by ambulance. He's really very weak. Not much more we can do for him here. I'll arrange everything. You should expect him around ten or so. But I'm glad your sons are there. You'll need all the help you can get. Do you have any questions?"

Grace shook her head.

"Grace?"

"No, that's fine. We'll expect him."

"One last thing," Travis added. "This can only be a

temporary arrangement, as I'm sure you'll understand. He's going to need constant care, probably beyond what you can do alone. As long as your sons are there to help out, he can stay home, but afterwards, well, we'll need to talk about having someone come in or perhaps find him a place in some home. I know I told you all that. I just want to make sure you understand. It's important."

"He'll never agree to that," she said, clearing her throat. "He calls that assisted dying, and I think he's right. I've heard such terrible stories about those places...."

"Now Grace, please. Let's cross that bridge when we come to it. I'm sure you'll agree."

She mumbled something and hung up. What else was there to say?

CHAPTER 12

The ambulance pulled up to the house at around 10:30, its heavy tires crunching the leaves and twigs that the storm had scattered on the driveway. A light mist had come up from the water and the obscured sunlight wrapped everything in a thick, damp cloak. A stiff breeze rippled the surface of the lake into regular pleats. Grace was sitting on a folding chair she had pulled outside waiting for his arrival. Wearing a heavy wool cardigan, she nonetheless shivered when she heard the vehicle make the turn off the main road and start onto the path that led up to the house. There was something about anticipation that was more frightening than the reality that she was going to face. She knew from experience that once she was busy, she would forget to be worried or upset. This trick of denying her emotions had always seemed to succeed, and she had learned that whenever she was tense or nervous, she would think of some task that needed her immediate attention. Of course Richard had watched this odd behavior long enough to know what it meant, and he would often laugh as she scurried about in their home in Chicago or the house here.

"Now what's bothering you?" he would ask. "Anything I did?"

And she would never tell him what it was because, indeed, it was often something that he had said or done or not done.

This morning had been like that, and after she had served breakfast to everyone, Nick had ordered her to sit down and rest.

"You're a whirlwind this morning, Mom," he said. "Stop it! I'm out of breath just watching you."

She laughed and then said, "All right, Nick. I'll just sit outside and wait for him to arrive."

That had been a half hour ago, and during that time, both Deck and Seth had come out to ask her if she was warm enough and whether it might be better to wait inside. But she had refused.

She stood up and walked around to the side to watch as the ambulance doors opened. She saw two orderlies jump out. They passed around to the rear and unlatched and swung the end panel back. Then they pulled out a metal ramp that clanged as it struck the driveway. Cautiously they maneuvered Richard, sitting in a wheelchair, down onto the hard surface. He smiled feebly at Grace when he saw her, and raised his hands slightly in greeting, and then closed his eyes.

Seeing him this way, she knew that something was changed about him. Yes, there was something different about him—the way he looked, perhaps, the slump of his body, his vacant expression. The tension and struggle seemed gone, replaced by something softer. She could sense it even from this brief glance, and she thought she knew what it was—she was sure, in fact: he seemed content to let the orderlies carry him, to tuck his feet onto the foot rest, and arrange his elbows on the rests of the chair—all without protest. She was certain what that meant: quite simply, he had given up. And that felt as if a heavy burden had now been shifted onto her. She had no idea what she would do.

"Wheel him over to the kitchen door," she said abruptly. "You'll have to manage the steps, but it shouldn't be difficult. This is the easiest way inside."

Seth, who had appeared suddenly behind her, pushed one of the men aside and helped the other pick up the chair to lift it through the kitchen door while she held it open for them.

The other orderly came up the steps and handed her a large package.

"It's medicine," he said, "and a list of instructions for his care. Nothing complicated, from what I understand. And the doctor said he'd be in touch."

Seth took the package and placed it on the kitchen table. Grace hesitated for a moment, wondering if she should tip the ambulance men, and then thought that, no, that would be odd and awkward, and it wasn't the same as giving a waiter in a restaurant something he expected and deserved.

"Thank you very much," she told them, and they walked outside to the ambulance and then backed it out of the driveway.

Nick and Seth maneuvered the wheelchair into the master bedroom and carefully lifted Richard onto the bed, propping him up with two pillows. After arranging the covers, they caught each other's eye. Seth shook his head very slightly, as if to flash some understanding between them—as if recognizing the difference in him, and after only one day in the hospital. His face was pale, almost the shade of a faded old yellow brief pad he was so fond of writing on, and when Seth hoisted him up, he seemed unable to exert any force to help. Smiling weakly, he said that he just wanted to sleep for an hour, that he would feel better with some rest, and they could talk then—to the whole family, because he had something he wanted to say.

"Do you think he wants to change his will?" Nick asked when he and Seth had returned to the living room.

"I doubt that very much," Seth said. "I don't know what he wants. We'll just have to wait."

It was late afternoon, almost dusk, when the family gathered in the living room. Richard had slept much longer than he intended. He was sitting in his wheelchair, a blanket tucked across his knees, when Seth wheeled him in. His face was flushed an unnatural color.

If he thought this might be some sort of dramatic entrance, when he looked at his sons and Grace, he saw only their curiosity and uncertainty. During the last few minutes, before he entered the room, he had tried to prepare what he wanted to say, but his thoughts were muddled, and he knew that his speech would be slurred and hesitant. But he needed to speak. There was so little time to set things right.

Before he could say a word, Grace, who was standing nervously at the side of the sofa, walked over and stood behind him, gently placing her hands on his shoulders. It was a reassuring gesture, and Richard hoped that she intended it to mean that whatever he was going to say, she would support him. It was almost as if the room had taken sides even before anything had been said.

"I hope you are feeling better," Lee said quietly. "I

mean all of us do. Thank God that you're back among the family. We prayed for you."

Richard just looked at her, shook his head, and then folded his hands in his lap.

"Well, I'm not much better," he mumbled. "Not at all. But at least it wasn't another heart attack this time."

Someone murmured something unintelligible.

"There's something I want to say to all of you before you ask," he began, clearing his throat. "I know I haven't got much time left. Dr. Travis told me this was a near miss, but next time, well, my heart just might give out."

No one said a word, but their silence seemed to energize him.

He took a deep breath and continued: "So I want to tell all of you that I refuse, absolutely refuse, to let anyone put me into some sort of house of the dying. I won't spend my last days surrounded by the stink of death! I want to be here, by the lake, with my wife, when my time comes. No matter what happens. I want you to promise me that."

"But Dad," Deck protested. "When we leave, how will Mom be able to cope? You're not thinking straight."

"Son," he said, "I've never been more determined in my life. What do I have three sons for if you can't figure out what to do among yourselves? Is it such an imposition to take care of your dying father?"

Nick looked at Deck and wondered if now was the moment he would say something about the will. But his brother remained quiet and just shook his head.

Finally, he said, "I don't know how."

"You'll think of something, Deck. You're supposed to be the resourceful one, aren't you?"

To Deck this seemed like a backhanded compliment,

and it stung him. He was tempted to blurt out something cruel. But he hesitated:

"I suppose Mom could hire someone to help out," he said. "If that's what you want. I wouldn't know how to do it. Maybe the doctor can recommend someone. It can't be too expensive down here."

Richard stared at his son, and then turned around to Grace still standing behind him.

"Can you wheel me back into the bedroom? I'm feeling tired, suddenly."

"I'll help," Seth said, quickly getting up off the sofa.

After the two disappeared into the hallway, Deck signaled to Nick that he wanted to talk to him outside.

When they were standing on the deck, both looking out over the lawn and the troubled waves eroding the placid surface of the lake, Deck turned to Nick and put his hand on his shoulder.

"I've come to a decision," he said. "I've decided to let the old bastard keep his money. Let them call it the Richard Collins Law School or whatever he wants it to be. I don't give a damn anymore. I give up."

"Now I'm puzzled. Did you ever actually intend to make trouble?" Nick asked.

"I don't know if I was ever really serious or not. Just really angry and hurt, I suppose. Wanting to do something. But now..."

"And now?"

"I can't stand seeing him like this. You know, when he's strong with that fucking stiff backbone of his, when he's being himself—the grand mufti of the law—well, I want to be his match. But now he's just pitiful, slumped over in a wheelchair with a blanket on his legs and a glazed look in his eyes. I guess I don't know myself well enough. I thought I could be just as tough as him. I thought: how good it would be to lock horns with him in court if that was possible. But I'm not. Can't go through with it, and I can't hurt Mom that way."

Nick was surprised at his brother's confession, and for a moment he recalled how disappointed he himself had been. The extra money would have changed his life, and he realized that he had begun to count on it. In his mind, he had already been house hunting, thinking of living with Mark in the two-bedroom split level he had purchased in his imagination. But he couldn't disagree. Deck had surely made the right decision. And he would forever be his brother's follower. He knew that.

"All right. Whatever you say. I'm just surprised that you changed your mind."

"Did you see him? Really see him?" Deck asked.

"I suppose I did. He was reaching out to us for help—of course, in his own way. The first time I can remember, in all my life, that the idea of 'helping out' wasn't just an order to do something, to fix something—some project or other he wanted assistance to complete."

"You got it right, Little Brother. You could see it as clearly as I could."

"So now what?"

"Well, tomorrow, first thing, early, Susan and I are going to drive back to Chicago. I've put her through too much already, and we need to head out. Lord only knows what she thinks of us—or me—with all the turmoil and fighting."

"She seemed OK to me. Maybe that's a good sign. If she can see you at your worst!"

Deck laughed: "Calm down now. Don't be rushing me into marriage, if that's what you're thinking. It's not going to happen. Just because I feel sorry for Dad, doesn't mean...."

"Then I guess I'll leave too," Nick said.

"Do you want a ride up-state? It wouldn't be terribly out of the way for us to drop you off."

"I don't think so," Nick said. "I like the train, and it gives me a chance to think about things."

"Suit yourself," Deck said. "I'm going inside to tell Susan and Mom and Dad."

"But what about the arrangements: The helper or visiting nurse or whatever to take care of him?"

"I guess they can sort that out themselves. I need to get back. But maybe you should stay on for a bit?"

"I can't," Nick said. "I've got classes. I've already taken too much time."

"I guess they watch you pretty closely, then, at your school."

"What the hell do you mean by that, Deck?"

"You know exactly what I mean."

"You're a rat, brother," he said. "You really are still a rat. And here, I thought you might have changed for a moment."

"Nope," Deck said, walking away. "Not possible, and now let's go back in. I think we'd both better say goodbye to him."

But when they returned to the living room it was empty.

"They probably put him back to bed. Don't want to disturb him now. So we can go in and say goodbye first thing tomorrow."

CHAPTER 13

Early the next morning, the two brothers met again in the living room.

"All right, Nick," Deck said. "It's your shot, first."

Nick shrugged, gave his brother an odd look and then headed to his father's bedroom. The door was open, and he entered quietly.

"Don't creep," Richard said, looking up. "I'm awake."

"I wasn't sure, Dad," Nick replied, edging close to the bed. "Are you comfortable?"

"Don't ask a foolish question, Nick. You never could say things straight out. So tell me...."

For a moment, Nick thought his father was demanding some sort of confession, to utter the words that he had never said to him, but he knew he couldn't, wouldn't, especially now. He wasn't sure what he should say. He couldn't just tell him goodbye. That word was so wrong, so hurtful and yet so provisional, as if he was just running an errand and would return in an hour. Goodbye was not right!

"I just wanted to tell you how sorry I am, Dad," he began, "and how happy that we've had these last moments together."

"It's all right, Nick," his father said, leaning forward slightly. "I understand." He raised his right arm and Nick grasped his fingers quickly in a clumsy handshake.

"Goodbye, Nick."

"Goodbye, Dad."

He watched Richard collapse back against the pillows, turned and left the bedroom.

"Are you crying?" Deck asked as he entered the living room.

Nick touched his hand to the corner of his eye, but said nothing. He didn't want to look at his brother, not at this moment, and he surely wasn't going to answer. Instead, he walked to the edge of the living room, opened the sliding door and stepped outside.

Deck hesitated for a moment because he wasn't sure exactly what he would say to his father and because this seemed so odd: to be in a parade of sons saluting their dying father. These last few days, he thought, had been miserable: the weather, the terrible announcement of the will, the odd feeling he had about Susan and her looks of disapproval, but most of all, his father dying. It hadn't really hit him before; he had been certain he wouldn't react; and now he was feeling an uncomfortable and strange sorrow. He had tried to be angry, because if he could hide his grief behind that, he might still be in control. But he could only think that death was an outrage. He was tempted to give in to its fury, but he couldn't. He was so like his father, so similar in everything, that this death seemed almost like his own.

When he entered the bedroom, his father's eyes were closed. As he moved closer, he fixed on the hand that lay on top of the covers, at his side, with its exposed blue veins crisscrossing the protruding tendons like the outlines of a bewildering map.

"Dad," he said quietly. "Dad."

Richard opened his eyes and tried to lean up on his elbows.

"You too," he said. "You, Deck?"

"Do you want some help?"

"No. Just leave it. And say what you have to say."

"I should be angry; I want to be angry," Deck began. "I should despise you for the will, for robbing us of our expectations. I was going to tell you that I planned to contest it in court—even though I know it's air-tight. You saw to that, didn't you! But just to hurt you. But I couldn't do it, and I won't. But I hate you.... I hate you for making me to be like you and I hate you for dying because a part of me goes with you. And I hate myself for feeling this sorrow that I can't control."

"Son," his father said, reaching out.

"I can't," Deck said, choking back a sob, and he hurried out of the room and into the bedroom where Susan was packing.

She had just closed her suitcase and was edging it onto the floor.

"I'll just be a minute more," she said to Deck. "I want to say goodbye to your mother."

"All right; don't be too long; I'll be waiting in the car."

She walked out of the bedroom and into the kitchen but found it empty, and then tried the living room. Through the large windows overlooking the lake, she could see Grace on a bench by the edge of the water. She was sitting motionless and Susan thought it was like a painting: a woman in a floral dress, a dappled pond, and morning light broken into rainbow streaks of pink and red by the fragile, thin clouds. It was lovely, and she hesitated to break the spell.

But she was determined and made her way outside onto the deck and down the path toward the lake. Grace turned to her when she heard the disturbance.

"How nice, Susan. Come sit with me for just a moment," she said. "I suppose you're going to tell me you're leaving, but it's such a lovely morning."

Susan said nothing but took her place as part of this portrait she imagined.

"Yes," she said, finally, "we're leaving in a minute. And I wanted to thank you."

"You mustn't," Grace said quickly. "I'm sorry you had to witness this awful time. And I have to apologize for my family. You must feel like you strayed into the last chapter of a tawdry novel."

"Not at all. My only regret is that I didn't get to know you better."

"That's very kind of you, but I'm just a walk-on in all the drama. It's their story, really."

Susan could almost feel the sadness and regret in her words.

"Do you mind if I ask you something?" she said.

Grace just nodded, and so she continued:

"I'm wondering, what do you plan to do now? I mean..."

"When he's gone?"

"Yes."

"I don't know. Maybe I'll leave. Sell this place."

"But where will you go? It's so lovely here. So quiet."

"I don't know yet. But I don't think I can stay."

"Is that because of the memories?"

"Yes, because of the memories," Grace exclaimed, taking her hand, "but not in the way you think. I'm talking about the memories of all the choices and compromises that brought us... me, to this place. You're very young, Susan, and you still have all the youthful illusions about love that glow so bright that they obscure everything else. But let me tell you a truth I've learned and I know it's an odd thing to say: but love is not an end in itself, only a beginning, and sometimes that can lead to a life of regrets. And when love fades, for whatever reason, all the things you ever wanted to do for yourself—and didn't accomplish—they come rushing back to haunt you as missed chances—all those unexperienced futures you once dreamed about. But your youth and everything else with it is gone."

Susan looked at Grace, trying to decide if she should embrace this elderly stranger, to hold her for a moment in her arms. She seemed so fragile.

"You must think I'm strange," Grace continued, "to confess such feelings to someone I scarcely know. But, you see, it's not your burden to understand and sympathize. And you can just dismiss what I say as the rantings of a distressed old woman, grieving for her dying husband and confused about what she will do when she's suddenly alone."

"Maybe a very wise old woman," Susan laughed.

"Perhaps. But tell me, my Dear, you and Deck?"

"I'll be honest with you, Grace, since you have been so frank with me; I had hopes once. I really did. That's why I agreed to this trip. But now I don't know."

She paused: "Actually, I'm pretty sure. I don't mean

that I discovered something terrible about him. It's just that I am seeing him in unguarded moments, and I don't like what I saw. I'm sorry. That sounds terrible. It's just that he's never let me see all of him. And now that I have, I..."

"That's all right, Susan," Grace said. "I know my sons, and I know everything good and bad about them. They're just who they are and I accept that."

They were silent for a moment, turning to the lake as a sudden breeze gathered up small waves that lapped against the shore; their motion lifted the edge of the boat, causing it to scrape audibly as it fell against the wooden dock.

"If you leave, do you know where you'll go?" Susan asked abruptly. "And what you'll do?"

"I don't know yet," Grace smiled. "Thank you for asking. But it won't be for a while and the next months or weeks or days or hours are going to be terrible. But I'll get through it somehow, and then, well, I have no idea. But I want it to be somewhere and something new; something I've always wanted to do. Things I've postponed for so long.."

Susan was silent for a moment and then she leaned over and kissed Grace on the cheek and took her hand in hers.

"I suppose I should leave now; Deck will be wondering," she said, getting up. "I think you're very brave!"

"All right. I'll sit for just a minute more," Grace said. "I'm so exhausted."

She watched the young woman walk up the steps, stride across the deck, and back into the house. Then she turned toward the lake again. The breeze had died down and the water had stilled, and the sun, much higher now, had plated the surface with an unbroken sheen of silver.

*

After the others had left, Lee and Seth sat with Grace at the kitchen table later in the afternoon, a teapot and empty cups set out in the middle.

"I just don't know what I'm going to do," Grace said, finally. "He's so difficult, even more so now. It's like he becomes more stubborn the weaker he becomes. Shouldn't it be the other way around? You'd think that, wouldn't you?"

Seth said nothing and so she continued:

"I suppose I should talk to Dr. Travis, as soon as possible, about somewhere we can put him." She shuddered at her own words and the idea of depositing someone in an institution as if they were just a coin pushed into a slot, without feeling or will.

"Or maybe he can suggest someone to live in and take care of him. He's too heavy for me to pick up," she continued. "And the expense of it! It hurts me to be thinking about costs. I know it shouldn't matter, but it does."

Seth reached over and took his mother's hand.

"There is another solution. I've talked to Lee about it, and I think it's perfect. We'll stay on. It won't be any bother for you because we can live in the camper, and I can help out with Dad. Lee will do the cooking and you won't have to do a thing."

"Oh, Seth. You know that won't work. He'll never agree to that."

Seth knew what she meant, although he didn't want to say it out loud: that of the three brothers, he ought to feel the least obligation and somehow that made it impossible. And there was the will which treated him almost as an afterthought.

And not even that—there were all the years of not quite belonging. But Seth had thought hard about it, and he knew that an obligation was an obligation, and he understood it was his duty as a son, no matter what kind of son he was, and however they had treated him, it was something he wanted to do. When he had discussed this with Lee about staying, she hesitated—reminding him about the position that was awaiting him in Florida. But he had insisted it didn't matter. If the elders decided to choose someone else because he couldn't be there, it was OK with him. Because he felt that God had finally found a way for him to square the circle of his errant life, and amend his unnatural and awkward place in the family. And the thought occurred to him at that moment that this was a strange deviation from the Biblical story of the Prodigal Son. He, the disfavored and estranged son, not the favorite, would return to be his father's keeper and his joy. Well, perhaps not his joy, but maybe he would eventually find acceptance. Yes, acceptance, he thought. He could finally do something that his father approved of.

"I'm going to tell him," Seth said. "And if he objects, well, I guess he's in no position to say no."

"You would do that? For us?" Grace said, looking at this odd man who had always been to her mind a strange intruder living in her home—this man who now seemed to be motivated by a faith that she had long ago rejected and could not even recall. He had always been someone who did not resemble her or Richard, and who bore none of their traits, and yet he was proposing something that her own flesh and blood would not consider for a moment. It made her wonder what, in all the troubled years of his youth, despite the terrible arguments with his father, and his failures to live up to their hopes, and his difference, his quirkiness—what made him now into the only one who seemed to care—in spite of everything?

"Are you sure, Seth? Don't you have obligations?"

"Yes, Mom, I sure do, and they're all right here with you. Nothing else matters. I'm going to talk to him now."

She watched him as he stood up and walked slowly out of the room. It occurred to her that even his gait was unusual and not at all like theirs, and yet there must be something inside him that belonged to them. She just wondered what that could be because she surely didn't know.

Seth entered the bedroom cautiously, in case his father was sleeping, but he saw that he was alert and staring at the doorway.

"How are you feeling, Dad?" Seth asked as he approached.

"Awful."

"I'm really sorry."

"Deck and Nick are leaving," he said. "They already came in to tell me. And I suppose you've come in here to say goodbye too."

"No. Lee and I are going to stay a while longer."

Richard leaned forward, trying to sit up straighter, and Seth reached over and propped him up.

"You didn't need to do that," his father said. "I can still manage a bit."

"Just helping out," Seth said.

"I don't need your help. And no reason for you to stay any longer."

"You do and we're going to; whatever you say."

His father closed his eyes and then opened them suddenly.

"You mustn't bother your mother. She's got enough to do without taking care of guests."

"I'm not a guest, Dad. And Lee and I are going to stay as long as we're needed. I won't let them take you away to some place you don't want to go. I wouldn't."

Richard looked at him curiously: "You'd do that for me? You'll stay?"

"Of course I will."

"Despite everything? Are you trying to cozy up to me when I'm too weak to object? I don't want that. I don't want your pity. Or is this some kind of strange religious thing? A pathetic attempt to convert me on my deathbed?"

"Come on, Dad, I'm just Seth, your son. Don't you recognize me?"

"Despite everything. The will?" He paused for a long time: "Did I make a terrible mistake?"

"No, you didn't, Dad. You just did what you thought was right. And that's exactly what I'm doing now. That's what you taught us, isn't it?"

Minutes passed while Seth watched his father fall back into a troubled sleep. Watching his chest rise and fall and listening to his heavy breathing, he thought about the barrier that had always seemed to stand between them, and wondered whether they would finally be able to breach it now or if it was too late. His father seemed so weak and the fight gone from him. And he could hardly remember what their struggles had been about. Maybe, he thought, it was just the simplest explanation of all: that he was adopted and he had never fit in.

His father stirred and opened his eyes.

"You're still here, Seth? What about Nick and Dexter?"

"Yeah, I'm here. Don't you remember? The others have already gone. Mom's still in the kitchen with Lee. At least that's where I left them."

Leaning on his elbows to sit up, his father said: "I doze off all the time now. Sometimes in the middle of a sentence. Especially when someone's talking. I'm sorry."

"That's OK."

He struggled up against the pillows to sit up, but waved Seth away when he leaned in to help.

"Will you do me a favor, son?" he said finally.

"Of course. Anything."

"Could you tell me again about that fishing trip we took? I've forgotten so much about it. The one where you caught that enormous pike. Do you remember that?"

"Are you sure?"

"Yeah. You never did get to the end. Some damned fool interrupted you. And you'll nudge me if I start to fall asleep, won't you?"

"It was a cloudy day and nothing was biting," Seth began, "and even the Indian guide was discouraged. You remember, don't you, Dad?

"Yes, Son, I remember."

"And then suddenly I felt an enormous tug on the end of my line... what a fighter that pike was!"

About Atmosphere Press

Founded in 2015, Atmosphere Press was built on the principles of Honesty, Transparency, Professionalism, Kindness, and Making Your Book Awesome. As an ethical and author-friendly hybrid press, we stay true to that founding mission today.

If you're a reader, enter our giveaway for a free book here:

SCAN TO ENTER
BOOK GIVEAWAY

If you're a writer, submit your manuscript for consideration here:

SCAN TO SUBMIT
MANUSCRIPT

And always feel free to visit Atmosphere Press and our authors online at atmospherepress.com. See you there soon!

About the Author

A true son born under the sign of Gemini, **JAMES GILBERT** has pursued twin careers. The first was Professor of History where he published eleven books on American Culture and retired as Distinguished University Professor at the University of Maryland.

The second is as writer of fiction and author of six—now seven—novels, three of which comprise the Amanda Pennyworth mystery series. Two of his short stories have won prizes from the F. Scott Fitzgerald Literary Contest. He currently resides outside Washington, DC.

Milton Keynes UK
Ingram Content Group UK Ltd.
UKHW030748071024
449371UK00006B/447